What would it be like to have her react to him with such obvious pleasure?

Where had that notion come from? Carter had left a horrible relationship. He didn't want another relationship yet when he and Ryan had finally settled into a good, steady life. Making sure Ryan felt safe and secure must be his focus. Yet, the thought of touching, kissing Liz had its appeal. Pulled at him. Maybe they could just be good friends.

In the small space his hip shifted into Liz's thigh. She stiffened against him. His body went into sensory overload. Soon he returned to his original position, but the awareness of their closeness didn't disappear.

Carter turned to her, putting his hand over hers. It was cold and he wanted to pull her to him and warm her up. "Please don't go."

Liz looked ready to bolt.

Carter pierced Liz with a look, afraid she might sneak away and unsure why it mattered that she stayed. "You'll wait for us?"

It took Liz longer than it should have for her to answer but she nodded. "I'll be here."

Dear Reader,

I loved writing this book. I've wanted to do so for a long time. To have a chance to create a love story in Mooresville, Alabama, was special, and to make it a Christmas event only made it extra special.

Mooresville is as picturesque as I describe it to be. I do add some fiction to the events, so don't go expecting those, yet the history is all true. The second I visited the historical town I started asking myself what characters I could dream up who would learn to love each other and make this place home. This book is about them.

I hope you enjoy Liz and Carter's story. I love to hear from my readers. You can reach me at www.susancarlisle.com.

Happy reading,

Susan

THE SINGLE DAD'S HOLIDAY WISH

———

SUSAN CARLISLE

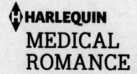

HARLEQUIN
MEDICAL
ROMANCE

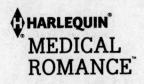

HARLEQUIN®
MEDICAL ROMANCE™

Recycling programs
for this product may
not exist in your area.

ISBN-13: 978-1-335-14976-3

The Single Dad's Holiday Wish

Copyright © 2020 by Susan Carlisle

Harlequin Enterprises ULC
22 Adelaide St. West, 40th Floor
Toronto, Ontario M5H 4E3, Canada
www.Harlequin.com

Printed in U.S.A.

Susan Carlisle's love affair with books began when she made a bad grade in mathematics. Not allowed to watch TV until the grade had improved, she filled her time with books. Turning her love of reading into a love for writing romance, she pens hot medicals. She loves castles, traveling, afternoon tea, reading voraciously and hearing from her readers. Join her newsletter at susancarlisle.com.

Books by Susan Carlisle

Harlequin Medical Romance

Miracles in the Making
The Neonatal Doc's Baby Surprise

First Response
Firefighter's Unexpected Fling

Pups that Make Miracles
Highland Doc's Christmas Rescue

Christmas in Manhattan
Christmas with the Best Man

Stolen Kisses with Her Boss
Redeeming the Rebel Doc
The Brooding Surgeon's Baby Bombshell
A Daddy Sent by Santa
Nurse to Forever Mom
The Sheikh Doc's Marriage Bargain
Pacific Paradise, Second Chance

Visit the Author Profile page
at Harlequin.com for more titles.

To Ryan

Thanks for joining our family.

CHAPTER ONE

DR. LIZ POOLE stood in the corner of the large room watching the other event attendees. *I have no business being here. A social butterfly, I'm not.* She wasn't any better now in interpersonal situations than she had been as a girl. Times like this she missed her sister, Louisa, the most. She'd been the one everyone wanted around, the life of the party. Yet Louisa wouldn't have come with Liz. This event she'd have considered dull.

Against Liz's better judgment and after the insistence of Melissa, her head nurse, Liz had decided to join the Christmas get-together. Melissa stayed on Liz about needing to go out more, be more social, meet someone. Often Melissa had teased her about turning into a hermit and becoming one of those cat ladies. Liz didn't even own a cat. To get Melissa off her back for a little while, Liz had forced herself to make an appearance at the party being held at the Riverside Country Club in Decatur, Alabama. Surely she would know a few people from working with them during one of the citywide events?

Liz took a sip of her sparkling pink drink so she'd have something to do. *At least it was good.* She scanned the small room. The group drinking cocktails appeared festively dressed in mostly red and green right down to the man with the plaid bowtie.

This party had been organized as a thank-you for the volunteers who had helped at festivals throughout the last year. One of the local businesses hosted it. Liz volunteered in the medical tent as often as her schedule would allow. Truly she wasn't as pitiful as Melissa and her mother believed.

Outside of her volunteer work, she had her chess and book clubs. She got out.

Dinner should be served in a few minutes. As soon as it was over, she'd slip out. Already fretting over having to make small talk during dinner, she searched for someone she knew to sit with. She could only hope her table companions would have partners on either side of them who would keep them occupied so she could just eat her meal.

She returned to her original thought of why she'd let Melissa talk her into coming. *Because it's advantageous for your job, your position in the community. You need to get out more,* Melissa's words singsonged through her head. No doubt her head nurse was correct but that didn't mean Liz found that a comfort.

Just the other day, her mother had once again lectured her on taking chances. Being her mother's only family and sole focus wasn't fun. Maybe by attending this event she would make her mother happy. Something Liz often found difficult to do.

The chairman of the city council's volunteer program tapped his glass, getting the crowd's attention. "I'd like to thank everybody for being here tonight." He looked directly at Liz.

No doubt he was surprised to see her since she'd been adamant she wouldn't be attending when he'd called the day before. He had invited her to a number of these events over the last few years and she'd declined them all.

"I hope everyone's looking forward to the holidays. We'd like to thank you for your service to the community during the past year and hope you consider helping us again." He twisted up his face and shrugged. "I also want to remind everyone that we have the Festival of Trees on the River event happening in a little less than two weeks. Those planning to help, please stay for a few minutes afterward. On that note, let's go in for dinner. It's buffet style, so feel free to fill your plates more than once."

Liz sighed. *There went her chance at a quick getaway.* She'd signed up to help in the medical tent during the festival's flotilla. Walking toward the double doors leading to the next room, she joined the line forming. She soon found herself sandwiched between two men. One was an older gentleman with a large belly and a red-tipped nose. She gave him a slight smile. Glancing at the tall man behind her, she found him busy talking to another man. He had a nice voice. Smooth, warm and inviting.

Her attention turned to the round dining tables. They had been covered in red cloths with greenery surrounding a candle. She needed to start her Christmas decorating soon. After the loss of her sister a little over a year ago and her father four years earlier, the holidays weren't as fun as they had been in the past. This year she planned to have more Christmas spirit than the last. The first holiday without a loved one was the most difficult.

A bump to her back made her lurch forward. She took a quick step to keep from falling as a firm hand grabbed her arm, steadying her. A zing of responsiveness ran through her.

"I'm so sorry. Are you all right?" The deep

voice she'd admired a few moments earlier said close to her ear.

Liz shivered as the heat of his hand seeped through the material of her blouse. "Yes, yes, I'm fine."

"Are you sure?" His intense green eyes studied her. "I didn't mean to almost knock you down."

"I'm okay. Really." He looked as if he were about her age. He towered over her. As an above-average woman in height, she appreciated his. For once in her life, she stood beside someone who fit her. She'd heard all the tall jokes in school, even knew she'd been rejected for dates because of her height. Add that to being "brainy" and high school had been painful. Louisa had saved her back then, but now she was gone.

"I'm glad. I apparently can't walk and talk at the same time. Or maybe it's that I don't look where I'm going." He offered her a charming smile.

Liz had no doubt he could use the same one to get out of a speeding ticket from a policewoman and succeed. It didn't hurt he was handsome with blond wavy hair trimmed tighter on the sides and longer on the top. He had the type of locks that invited a woman to run her fingers through them.

Oh, my goodness, she really had lost her mind.

Over a white shirt, he wore a burgundy cable sweater. Tan slacks hugged trim hips and dark brown suede shoes finished his outfit. All in all, he was the complete package of a fine-looking male.

He indicated with his hand. "We'd better move ahead or the line will start going around us."

"Oh," she gasped. She'd been staring. A gap had grown between her and the man ahead. Liz hurriedly closed the space.

The man with the plaid bowtie walked past them with his plate full.

"Not everyone can carry one of those off," the man behind her whispered, as he stepped up beside her.

Liz giggled and nodded. "I agree."

"By the way, I'm Carter Jacobs." He offered his hand.

A large comfortable hand surrounded hers as she took it. "Liz Poole."

"Nice to bump into you. I mean uh…meet you." He grinned.

"You too." He certainly could charm. She

stepped forward, making sure a break didn't form again. When she stopped, she glanced back.

Carter's gaze returned to her. "So, do you come to these sorts of things often?"

That question made Liz grin. He could only be sincere because that come-on line must be the oldest of them all. "Truthfully, this is the first one I've been to."

"It's my first, as well. I'm sort of new to town."

This time she suppressed a laugh. Was he for real or was his entire vocabulary nothing but pickup lines? "Welcome to Decatur. I hope you're happy here." Liz groaned to herself. She had started to sound as lame as him.

"My grandparents used to live here so I'm familiar with the area."

She nodded. "I was born and raised here."

"Then I guess you know all the ins and outs of living here." He looked directly at her.

Her cheeks grew warm. Was he flirting with her? If he was, she liked it. "I don't know about that."

He glanced around the room. "Do you volunteer often?"

"Three or four times a year. Usually at large events where a doctor's needed."

"You're a doctor?" A note of surprise hung in his voice.

"I am an otolaryngologist."

"An ENT. My son spends his fair share of time with one of those despite his father being an internist."

"You're a doctor, as well. Small world." Now she was the one amazed. In the medical world, she felt confident. "Sometimes the most you can do is put in tubes. Infections can be hard to cure otherwise."

"So I've learned. But like most parents, I don't want to go there even if my training says differently. Why haven't I met you before? I've worked a few events."

"I've been on call the last two so that might be why." Was he coming on to her? Even if he wasn't, it was still nice to have a man pay her some attention. That alone made the awkwardness of coming tonight worth it.

Liz arrived at the stack of plates at the end of the buffet table. Taking one, she started down the long table, filling her plate with food. Carter followed the line to the other side. Liz finished well before he did. She looked back to find him. Not wanting to appear presumptuous that he might want to sit with her, she went looking for a place without waiting on him. A woman she knew called her over to her table. Liz took the last open seat. She noticed Carter looking her way before he moved to another area of the room.

Carter exited the building, zipping up his jacket against the cool December weather. A breeze rolling in off the nearby Tennessee River always made it feel colder. He ran his hand into his trouser pocket, searching for his keys.

The parking lot was almost empty. His SUV and a small compact car were all that remained on this side of the building. As he walked, he saw the woman he had brushed against in the dinner line, the one with the pretty smile, sitting in the driver's seat. She appeared perplexed.

A grinding noise came from her car. Carter approached a little slower. The sound came again. Walking wide around the car, he circled toward the front so that she could see him. He raised a hand in an effort not to frighten her.

Her eyes widened. He went to her window and tapped, making a circular motion with his hand for her to roll it down. She hesitated, then did as he requested. "I didn't want to scare you. Can I help?"

"I don't know what's wrong. It just won't start." Frustration rang loud and clear in her voice. "Everything was fine when I got here."

"Try it one more time." Carter kept his voice calm while hoping he could actually help.

The same grinding noise reverberated around the car. Liz gave him a look of expectation as if he'd have the answer. Carter wished he could give her more encouraging news. He shook his head. "It's not the battery because it wants to turn over. I wish I could tell you more. I'm a much better doctor than I am a mechanic."

She huffed, hers lips thinning. "I appreciate your help. I'll call the auto service and have them come."

"It's too cold for you to wait out here."

"I'll go back inside." She gathered her purse.

"I saw them locking up on my way out. Even the caterers are gone. I can't leave you here by yourself."

"I'll be fine. It shouldn't take the tow truck too long to come."

Was she afraid of him? Outside of their short conversation, they really were strangers. "You might be surprised. Why don't you give them a call while I wait?" He stepped away, giving her some privacy.

She picked up the phone. Shoving his hands into his pockets, he rocked back on his heels while she talked.

"Really? It's going to take that long?" Liz said into the phone. Soon she hung up.

He winced. "That didn't sound good."

She dropped her phone into her purse and gave him a disgusted look. "It wasn't. It's going to be over an hour before they can get here." She looked past him, then at the dark building, her attractive face drawing up with concern.

"You don't need to stay here by yourself. It's already dark." His lips tightened. "My teenage babysitter has to be home soon since it's a school night. I know we don't know each other well but I wish you'd let me take you home. I just need to stop by my house for a sec."

She shook her head. "That's not necessary. I'll just stay here and lock the doors."

"And freeze to death." He couldn't be that scary. "Come on, it's too cold for you to do that." He stomped his feet to warm them, emphasizing his point. "I promise I'm a good guy. You at least know me better than you do the wrecker driver."

She bit her bottom lip, looking unsure. "I don't know."

"So you do know the wrecker driver?"

She gave him a quizzical look, then a slight smile. "No, I don't know him."

"See, you do know me better. Do you have

someone you can call to come pick you up who can be here in a few minutes?" Carter checked his watch. He should be going.

"Not really. My mother's out this evening and my nurse lives thirty minutes away." Her pitiful look tugged at him.

"Come on then. You've no choice. I'll need to take you home. If it'll make you feel better, you can call someone and tell them who I am, where we're going and what's going on. Leave the phone on the whole time."

Liz exhaled, looking over her shoulder at the building again. "I'll call my nurse."

Carter listened as she explained her predicament.

"Melissa wants to know your home address."

He gave it to her. Glancing at him, she lowered her eyelids and said into the phone. "Yes."

If the light hadn't been so dim, he could have confirmed his suspicion that she'd blushed. What had her nurse asked her?

"I'll call you the minute I get home. Promise." She hung up, then gathered her purse and stepped out of the car, locking it. "On our way I'll call the tow truck and tell them where to take the car. I don't live far. About twenty minutes from here."

"My house is a little farther but I'll make it

as short a trip as possible." He started toward his SUV.

She hesitated. "I'm still not sure about this."

"It's either go with me or I'll call the police and have them come." He hated having to blackmail her but his conscience wouldn't let him leave her, and he had Ryan to see about, as well. His son had been abandoned by his mother one too many times and Carter refused to let Ryan worry his father might do the same. Keeping his word to his son was of supreme importance.

Liz's shoulders lowered in defeat. "That's not necessary. I'll come. I just hate having to put you out."

"It's not a problem." They continued toward his SUV. "We'll get it all worked out." Carter unlocked the car, held the front passenger door open until she climbed in and closed it behind her.

Minutes later they headed down the highway. She called the motor service, then an unsure silence settled over them. Carter glanced over to find her sitting rigid with her hands clasped in her lap as if she were ready to spring out at a moment's notice.

Went he first met her, he'd been struck by her height. She had super long legs. The kind that could wrap around a man. Ho, that wasn't a thought he should be having about a woman he didn't really know. Had he been without sex for so long he'd started to lose his mind? That aside, he liked that he didn't have to bend down to talk to her. Even though she wore a sedate black pants suit, he could tell she had some nice mature curves. Beneath the jacket, she had on a red shirt that she filled out nicely with full breasts.

She'd appeared insecure when they first met. He'd actually been surprised she spoke to him. He liked the way she giggled. All girlie-like. It rippled around him, urging him to join in her humor. He'd not shared laughter with a woman in too long. "By the way, where do you live?"

"In Ridgewood. In this direction but you turn right just down here." She pointed north at a major intersection.

"We're not that far apart. I live in Mooresville."

"I've heard of it, but I've never been there."

He sensed her looking at him. "If you blink, you'd miss it. It's just across the river and a little way off the main highway. It won't take long to get there. I'll have you home soon. Promise."

Liz fell quiet again. Something about her made him believe she'd never gone off with a man she didn't know. She didn't strike him as someone who picked up men in bars. In fact, he'd call her wary of others. As if she might have been hurt one too many times by people.

He'd also noticed she had rich brown hair and wide dark expressive eyes. He couldn't think of any reason why a man wouldn't want to pick her up. Even him, if he were looking for someone, which he wasn't. His ex-wife had seen to that. Peace and security were what he wanted. He and Ryan had found that between just the two of them. But would it be so bad to have someone to spend time with who could talk about more than the latest cartoons?

He shot glances at her as they crossed over the river bridge. He should focus on the road. "So, where's your office located?"

"It's downtown close to the hospital. It's in one of the older brick medical buildings that has been renovated."

"I know the ones. Mine's in the medical park about a mile away. I can't believe we haven't met before now."

"It happens." She went quiet once again.

"We're almost there." He turned off the main highway.

Making a right, he drove about a mile and came to the historical marker that read Mooresville. He glanced at Liz to find her leaning forward, looking out the windshield with interest. "You can't see much because we don't have streetlights. You need to come back when it's daylight. It's really a great place."

"I'll have to do that. Why did you decide to buy here when you came to town?"

"I bought my grandparents' house when they decided to move to Florida. I wanted to bring my son up in a place where the neighbors knew each other." He chuckled. "I might've gotten carried away. This place is tiny, but it has a big caring vibe for sure."

"It looks like a safe and secure place for a family. What's your wife going to think when you show up with a strange woman?"

"I'm divorced. Four years." That had become easier to say with each year.

"I'm sorry."

Carter nodded. He wasn't. Outside of having Ryan, his marriage had been toxic at best. A mistake not to repeat. Making a left around the large township square, he then turned again to the right and made an immediate left into his pebbled parking area behind his house.

"What a great house." Liz cocked her neck upward to see his two-story home out the side window.

He grinned. "I'm pretty crazy about it. Even if it can be drafty this time of year and it needs some work in a couple of areas. As my grand-parents got older, it became more difficult for them to do upkeep. I've been slowly getting things back in order." He opened the door. "I won't be but a few moments. Would you like to come in or wait here?"

"I'll just wait here."

"Okay, I'll be right back." Carter shut the door behind him.

Liz watched Carter lope to the back steps. Only desperation could have made her go off with a stranger. Or almost stranger. Carter couldn't be all bad if he lived in this community.

She looked at the house again, a clapboard building painted white. She guessed it must be around a hundred years old. She'd glimpsed a front porch before he had made the turn onto the second street that led to the back of his house. The windows were tall and light shone out of those along the back, giving her a view of a brick patio surrounded by a wooden trellis. A firepit sat in the middle with chairs around it, including a child-sized one.

Good as his word, Carter soon headed her way. He had a young boy wrapped in a blanket in his arms and a teenage girl following him out the door. Liz turned and watched Carter set the child in a booster seat behind the driver's seat. The boy, who already showed signs of looking like his father, now studied her.

Carter must have sensed his son's curiosity because he glanced at her. "Ryan, this is Dr. Poole. She's a new friend. Her car wouldn't start so we're going to take her home."

"Hello, Ryan. It's nice to meet you." Liz gave him her best reassuring patient smile.

"Hi," the boy said after a pause.

"Buckle up, Ryan." Carter closed the door.

Ryan buckled in as Carter climbed behind the steering wheel.

The girl took the seat behind Liz. "Liz, this is my sitter, Betsy."

Liz twisted to see the girl. "Hello."

The girl offered her a slight smile.

She reminded Liz of herself at that age. Painful.

"Okay, everyone in. Betsy, I'll drop you off first and Liz, you'll be next. Then it's back to bed for you, Ryan."

Liz shoulders sank. "You had to get him out of bed. I'm sorry. I should've just stayed with my car."

"Don't worry about it." He reached over and patted her shoulder but quickly removed his hand. Still, a tingle ran through her. "He wasn't asleep, and he thinks this is a great adventure."

"Daddy, can we get an ice cream on the way back?" the boy asked.

Carter chuckled. She liked the sound. It reminded her of the ripples of an echo, smooth and easy.

"I think it's a little too late for ice cream. How about some hot chocolate before you go to bed again?"

There was a pause. Liz glanced back. The boy appeared to give the idea some thought. "Okay, but I like ice cream better."

Carter chuckled again and turned into a subdivision. "I do too." At the second drive, he pulled in and stopped. "Betsy, thanks for tonight. I'll call you about watching Ryan while school is out."

The girl said softly, "Okay."

"Also, be sure to tell your parents they're welcome to come to our community Christmas event Saturday evening. See you later."

"Bye, Betsy," Ryan said.

"Bye." Betsy climbed out of the SUV.

Carter waited until the girl went inside, then backed out.

Liz said, "I appreciate you being a taxi driver for me."

"I would've had to bring Betsy home anyway. You're the one being patient about getting home."

"I didn't have much of a choice." She hesitated. What made her say something that ill-mannered? "I'm sorry. That didn't sound very grateful."

He looked at her. "I know what you mean." His attention returned to the rearview mirror. "How were things tonight, Ryan?"

"We watched TV and ate pizza. Do you like pizza?"

"You know I do," Carter replied.

"No, I mean her."

Liz turned to see him pointing a finger in her direction. "I do very much."

"What kind?" the boy asked.

"Almost any kind, but I especially like a meat lover's. What's your favorite?"

"Cheese."

She smiled at the boy's enthusiastic answer.

"I hate to interrupt this conversation, but I need to know where you live." Humor filled his voice as he drove toward town again.

"At the third light, turn right," Liz told him.

Ten minutes later they were at the gated entrance to her townhouse complex. She told Carter the code and he punched it in. Somehow the place she lived seemed sterile compared to his house. As if she were marking time instead of living. "Mine's the third one on the right."

He pulled to the curb in front of it and turned off the SUV. "Let me walk you to the door."

"That's not necessary. You shouldn't leave Ryan." Liz located her keys in her purse. "Thank you again for bringing me home. What do I owe you for your trouble?"

He leaned back as if she had hit him. "Nothing."

"I need to do something to say thank-you. Would you and Ryan like to go out for pizza on Saturday? My treat."

"I do!" came from the back seat.

Carter shook his head. "That sounds nice, but we can't."

Disappointment washed over her. *That figured.* For once she'd put herself out there and what happened? She'd been turned down. It shouldn't hurt but it did.

"We've a community event and we both have to be there. Hey, why don't you join us? Ryan and I'd like you to be our guest."

She couldn't do that. Go to a neighborhood party with Carter. What would people think? Would people assume she and Carter were in a relationship? "I'm supposed to be doing something nice for you."

"It's a community Christmas Stroll. We have

a potluck/grill-out meal just for the neighbors beforehand, then the public's welcome to tour a couple of open houses and the Brick Church. There's caroling. I think you'd enjoy it."

At least that sounded better than what she'd imagined. Carter made it sound interesting, and she'd like to see Mooresville in the daylight. "I don't know. I don't want to be in the way."

Carter turned to her with an eager look on his face. "I promise you won't be. There'll be plenty of people around who don't live in Mooresville. Come join us. You'll be glad you did."

"Should I bring something?" Was she really thinking of attending?

"If it'll make you feel better, then bring something. If you decide to come, make it around three. We eat early so we can have everything cleaned up before the program."

"I'll think about it. I may have to work. I really appreciate the ride." She climbed out of the SUV. "Bye."

As she went inside Carter pulled away from the curb. This evening hadn't turned out at all as she had expected. To her surprise that rather excited her.

CHAPTER TWO

THE NEXT MORNING Liz still puzzled over having asked Carter and Ryan out for pizza. It wasn't like her to invite strangers to dine with her. However, she'd wanted to say thank-you to Carter in some way after he'd gone to so much trouble to help her. The impulsive pizza invitation was out of her mouth before she'd thought.

More mystifying was that she was actually considering going to the community event. She did want to see Mooresville. And Carter. It had been a long time since she'd been around a man that interested her.

Melissa, sporting a pink streak in her hair and wearing purple scrubs, started quizzing Liz about the night when Liz opened the door to get into Melissa's car.

"So, did you find yourself a knight in shining armor?" Melissa laughed as Liz shook her head and closed the door. "I told you going to the party would be good for you, Liz. Tell me the details, girl. Details. You said he was good-looking. How good-looking is he?"

"He's tall—"

"Aw, come on. You can do better than that. Does he have dreamy eyes? A sweet butt?" Melissa looked over, wiggling her brows. "Big hands?"

Liz laughed.

"Well?"

Heat surged up her neck. "Okay, he has all of that."

"Oh, wow. The full package. You go, girl," Melissa crowed.

Liz huffed. "It wasn't like that."

"Who says it can't be?"

"He just gave me a ride home, that's all. He did invite me to a community get-together on Saturday, but I don't know if I'll go."

Thankfully they were at a light as Melissa glared at her. "Are you crazy? You go Saturday to that community thing and he'll find out how wonderful you are and the next thing you know, you're in love." Melissa's excitement could easily turn contagious.

Liz looked back at her. "You need to give up reading those romance novels during lunch."

"And you need to start believing there's someone out there who can give you a happily-ever-after. Show your mother you're as special as your sister was."

Too pragmatic for such nonsense, Liz remembered vividly the reality of being invisible when Louisa was around. Her sister had always been the center of attention. If Louisa wasn't, she made sure she was. Liz had been okay with that because Louisa had pulled her along into the crowd. With Louisa gone, life had changed in that aspect. It was much harder to join in when Liz had to do it on her own. If Liz went on Saturday, she'd have to do it all on her own. The idea disturbed her.

Just before the lunchbreak the receptionist told Liz she had a call on hold from a Dr. Jacobs.

Carter. With hands shaking, Liz picked up the phone. "This is Dr. Poole."

"It's Carter. I just wanted to make sure you made it to work with no trouble."

She cleared her throat. It was really sweet of him to check on her. "Thanks, that's nice of you. I did. My nurse picked me up this morning."

"Great. And your car made it to the shop, as well?"

"It did." She wasn't used to receiving this type of attention. Nice, but unnerving at the same time. Maybe being new in town, Carter needed a friend and had latched on to her. "My mom's coming to pick me up this afternoon so I can go get a rental for a few days."

"Good. I'm glad you have someone you can depend on."

Had someone disappointed him?

"I also wanted to invite you again to come on Saturday. It'd be a great way to learn about Mooresville."

Why did he care so much if she attended? They had just met. He made it sound important that she come. "I'll try."

"Good. The community committee could use a fresh opinion on what we're trying to do."

There it was. His interest lay in her ideas. Hadn't he been just as enthusiastic about Betsy's parents coming? She wasn't sure if that made her feel better or worse. She'd like him to ask her to join him because he wanted to see her. What an interesting notion.

"I'll see you Saturday then."

He made it difficult for her not to go. After all the trouble he had gone through for her the night before, she did feel obligated to do something nice for him. As of right now, unless something came up, she'd attend. "I'll try, unless I have to be on call at the last minute. I'm sorry. I've got to go. I've patients waiting."

"Same here. Hope to see you Saturday. Bye."

Liz hung up and sat there for a moment. She'd spent most of her life in her sister's shadow, unnoticed by others unless Louisa pointed Liz out. She'd gotten used to making little effort because she didn't have to. She'd found out early on that people found her intelligence off-putting. So why did Carter *see* her? Whatever the reason, it felt good. And unnerving. Did he want something she didn't know about? Could he just be a nice guy? Or maybe he *was* a nice guy. Whatever the reason, she'd take it while it lasted.

She mentioned the call to Melissa, who jumped around. "You have to go. I've never understood why you hold yourself back when you're one of the most attractive and accomplished women I know. You need to work on believing that too."

Unsure how to respond, Liz looked at her. Had she really been hiding away? Liz had been living as she always had. Only now Louisa wasn't there to pull her along. Had it become easier just to not make an effort to get to know anyone new?

Melissa continued on, unaware of the turmoil her words generated in Liz. "I know what we'll do to help make it happen. Friday, since we're closed in the afternoon, we're going to go get haircuts and have our nails done. Then we'll see about buying you a new top to go with your jeans."

"I have paperwork to do." To prove it Liz looked down at her electronic device.

"Paperwork can wait. You need a little confidence builder. When was the last time you went out with a man?"

Liz hesitated to confess. "A couple of years ago."

"Wow. You need to make this one count. You like him, don't you?"

She did. More than she believed she would or wanted to. Liz nodded.

"Then make an effort. Do something for yourself for a change. You help people here every day, volunteer your weekends away, play chess with the elderly and jump when your mother says to. For once, think about yourself." Melissa sounded pleading and annoyed at the same time.

She pulled Liz to a nearby mirror. Her hands remained on Liz's shoulders as she looked over one. "Stop a minute and look at yourself. Would it hurt for you to try a little harder? Come on, Liz. Take a chance. Be fearless for once. You can do it." She grinned. "Think about how nice you told me his smile is."

Now Melissa teased her. Liz hesitated a moment before she sighed. "Okay. For you."

Melissa's eyes met hers in the mirror. "No. For you."

"Okay. For me too." Liz stepped back.

"You've got to start thinking about yourself. Get out more. Let people know the real you. Get your mother out of your head. Start taking some chances. Live a little."

Had Liz really become so unresponsive to men that she acted like a troll hiding away? That hadn't been her intent. She'd try. Really try.

Liz spent the rest of the week working up the nerve to take Carter up on his invitation.

Saturday afternoon Liz reminded herself again to pay close attention to her driving instead of the thumping of her heart as she neared Mooresville. It wouldn't do for her to cause an accident. *She was doing this.*

Just as Carter had said, Mooresville did look different in the daylight. She turned off the main road and faced a large grassy square where a huge redbrick building set. Making the turns she remembered, she traveled toward Carter's house. She pulled into the parking area behind it. Louisa would have found nothing about Mooresville exciting. Her interests had been in the new and exciting. Liz loved everything about the old buildings. Louisa would've hated them. She turned off her engine.

After knocking and finding no one at home, Liz gathered her pie plate and walked to the front of the house. She stopped to look at it closer. The porch looked comfortable and inviting. A place where a family could sit on a sunny afternoon and visit with friends. Nothing about this place could be called cold or cookie-cutter like the place she lived.

A Christmas wreath sporting a big red bow hung on the front door. Smaller, matching wreaths hung in the center of the windows on each side of the door. Two pots filled with greenery and large pine cones set on either side of the door. Pillows covered in a red-and-green holly print were stationed in the wicker chairs on one side of the porch, while on the other they were propped in the corner of a swing. Carter had been busy decorating. Interesting personality trait in a single father. One she hadn't expected.

She started across the central square toward a brown clapboard building. There people mingled around while others were busy setting up a food table covered by a green cloth. She passed a group of kids playing tag. Ryan ran among them. He stopped to study her for a moment. Liz smiled and waved, then concentrated on making steps toward the group of adults in spite of her apprehension.

If she turned around now, Carter would never know she had been there. Except Ryan would tell him. She'd handled medical emergencies that hadn't generated this amount of trepidation. Liz squared her shoulders with determination and continued.

"Liz, you made it." Carter came to meet her. His bright smile suggested he was both excited and somewhat surprised to see her. A large apron with a picture of a grill on fire covered his green fleece pullover making his eyes more brilliant. She blinked. Her heart raced. Below that he wore jeans and sports shoes on his feet. Carter looked happy, healthy and all male. Everything about him tempted her to dream of what-if.

"I did." She looked around at the people who watched them. They all had smiles on their faces. Liz returned them.

One middle-aged woman stepped forward. "Let me take that."

Liz released the pie plate with a smile of appreciation.

"You look nice. Have you had your hair cut since I saw you?" Carter asked.

"I did." She was glad now that she'd spent that time on her nails and hair. Carter noticing gave her a boost of confidence.

He watched her carefully. "You look nice."

"Hey, Carter. You better get back over here before these sausages burn," a man behind one of the two grills called.

"Come over here and talk to me while I *man* the grill." Carter turned with a grin.

Liz followed, unsure what she'd talk to him about.

He picked up tongs and moved to stand in front of a grill. "Hey, everyone, this is Liz Poole. I invited her to join us today."

A few people called hello. She nodded, making eye contact as much as she could.

"I'm really glad you decided to come." Carter moved around a couple of sausages he'd added to those already over the fire. "What kind of pie did you bring?"

"Apple."

"Aw, my favorite. Put some ice cream on it and I've found heaven." He made a sound of pleasure that pulled low in her body.

"Everything leads back to ice cream for a man," Liz said before thinking. She hoped he wouldn't take it as criticism. "My father loved it."

"If it doesn't, it should," Carter quipped and returned his attention back to his cooking.

"This is an interesting building." Liz studied the long narrow wooden structure with doors trimmed in red on each end. The screen doors wore greenery wreaths with plaid bows. Beside one door, an American flag hung from a pole attached to the building. In front of it was a small brick area with two benches facing each other.

"It's the post office. One of the four original buildings from 1818." A proud note rung in his voice.

"Carter, do we have another pan for the hot dogs?" the man at the other grill asked.

With Carter's attention diverted, Liz studied the area with its road around the huge square. She could now see that the township had been laid out in a grid. There were two main center squares. Off those were two streets on either side. Not as many houses were on Carter's side of the square. On the opposite were a number of buildings with picket fences, but there were still open lots. Undoubtedly those structures had gone with time. Charming was the only word she could find to describe the historic town.

"Ow," came a male yelp of pain.

Liz turned to see a man doubled over in

front of a large pot. Hot oil streamed around him. She hurried to him, her focus on nothing but the man. Sweat broke out in the center of her back. "Are you all right?"

Others circled them. The man yanked at his sweatshirt, trying to remove it.

"Let me help." Carter started pulling on his shirt. Beneath it was another long sleeve knit shirt. The injured man pushed at it.

"Don't do that!" Liz cautioned. "Does anyone have a pocketknife?" Someone handed her one and Liz gave it to Carter. "Cut it back."

He nodded and turned to the man. "John, I'm going to cut your shirt. Karen'll have to get over it."

As Carter went to work on the shirt, Liz held it away from John's skin.

"Liz, pull it open and away as I cut," Carter instructed.

She did as he told her, being careful not to touch the man's burned skin.

John hissed and immediately jerked when air hit the burn.

"Please be still. I need to see it. I'm a doctor too," she informed him.

The man stilled. His other hand moved to touch.

"Don't touch. We don't want the skin to

come off. It's your protective covering. It helps prevent infection."

Carter removed the fabric of his shirt. The middle-aged man winced. An angry burn extending the length of his forearm came into view.

She grimaced. "We need to get some ice on this."

A woman volunteered, "I'll fetch an ice bag."

"This must be cleaned and bandaged." She looked at Carter. "We're going to need soap and water. Bandages."

"We'll go to my house." Carter turned. "Stan, see to the grill, please."

The woman returned with a bag of ice large enough to cover the burn.

Liz placed the bag over the burn area. "Keep that on it. I know it'll be uncomfortable but it's important."

The man stoically nodded and brought his arm to his chest.

"Okay, John, let's go get you fixed up." Carter looked around. "Where's Karen?"

"She's at the house, putting together some last-minute food." John's words were tight from pain.

The lady who had gotten the ice called, "I'll let her know what happened and where you are."

Liz and Carter walked on each side of John toward Carter's house.

"Ryan," Carter called. "Find Mrs. Wilson if I'm not back by the time dinner's ready."

The boy gave them a curious look. "Yes, sir."

They entered Carter's home through the unlocked front door. Liz would never dream of leaving her place open to anyone at any time. Inside, they continued down a narrow hall to the back of the house. Liz dodged a waist-high table sitting against a wall as she hurried across gleaming wood floors. The three of them stopped in front of a white country sink.

"We need some dish detergent to cut the grease and a towel." Liz turned on the water, making sure it was as cool as possible.

"John, this is Dr. Liz Poole." Carter opened the cabinet beside the sink and pulled out a plastic bottle of blue liquid. He sat it on the counter within her reach.

"Hi, John. I know you're in pain. You've a bad burn here. Carter and I are going to get it cleaned and bandaged up. Soon you should feel better. Carter, we're going to need a first aid kit too. Do you have one?"

"I do. Can't have a seven-year-old child without one." He left the room.

"John, I'm going to need to get the oil off

your arm. This is probably going to hurt but I'll be as gentle as possible. I'll also be as quick as I can. I've got to be extra careful or I'll open up that blister. I don't want to do that. The main thing with burns is to protect you from infection. I can't stress that enough."

She scooped water on the man's arm, then lightly dribbled the dish liquid. Using her palm, she carefully applied light pressure to the red skin with a blister over it. As gently as possible, she worked to remove the oil without damaging the skin. Carter returned with the first aid kit and stood on the other side of John.

The man groaned.

"I'm sorry. I know this isn't any fun but it's necessary." Liz worked as quickly as she could.

"I shouldn't be such a baby," the older man said.

She smiled at him. "No babies here. Burns are painful and yours is a big bad one."

Slow and easy, she focused on removing the oil, continually adding water and liquid soap until satisfied the area was as clean as she could make it.

Carter reached across the counter, pulled out a drawer, grabbed a dry towel and handed it to her. She blotted it dry enough that it would quickly finish air-drying. By the time she finished, Carter had the first aid kit open.

He squeezed some antibiotic cream out of a tub on to a four-by-four square and placed that over a section of the arm and repeated the action until all the injured area had been covered. "The cream should keep the gauze from sticking when the bandage is changed."

Carter then pulled out a roll of gauze, opened it and started wrapping it around John's arm until all the damaged area had been covered.

At a sharp knock on the front door, Carter called, "Come in."

Rapid footsteps soon followed. A small white-haired woman with bright red cheeks rushed into the kitchen. "John, what have you done?"

"Karen, he's fine. He just has a grease burn on his forearm," Carter assured her. "We have it all protected now but he needs to keep ice on it until the pain goes away."

"Mary said you need clothes. I brought you another shirt and jacket." Karen studied her husband as if making sure he had no other injuries.

"Good. Why don't you help him dress? Liz and I'll get things cleaned up here." Carter looked over at the older couple and smiled.

"Just be careful not to touch his arm any more than necessary."

John and Karen moved over to the wooden dining table near a rear window.

"They both need a few moments together," Carter whispered to Liz. "They've been married forty-five years. Are completely devoted to each other."

"I understand." What would it be like to have that type of relationship, commitment? Liz would like to have that. So far that hadn't been in the stars for her. After glancing at Carter, she picked up the bag of ice in the bottom of the sink and then dropped the dripping mess. "We're going to need another ice pack."

"I've just the thing." Carter went to the freezer compartment of the refrigerator and pulled out a bag of peas. "At least they'll be going to a good cause since Ryan won't eat them."

"I'm not a big fan of peas either. Wrap it in a dish towel and it'll be perfect."

Carter pulled out the drawer again and removed another towel. "Why don't you prepare this while I clean up our mess?"

His hand touched hers as he handed them to her. That current she'd felt before went through her. She managed to get out, "Okay."

Soon John and Karen joined them.

Liz said, "John, you need to keep some ice on that arm. It'll help with the pain and keep down swelling." She placed the improvised ice pack over the burned area. "Also, I'd suggest you have Carter do the changing of your bandage tomorrow. After that, I'm sure Karen can handle it. And no more cooking for you for a while." Liz smiled at him.

"Those doctor's orders sound like good ones. I have some pain medicine for you." Carter handed the man two white pills. "Take these now." He offered the man a glass of water. "I suggest you also take something before going to bed. It'll help you sleep. If you have any concerns, you call and I'll come running."

"My goodness, it's nice to have such good doctors looking after John." The concern on Karen's face had eased.

"I'm glad I could help," Liz said.

"Same goes for me." Carter patted Karen on the shoulder. "Now, why don't you take John to get something to eat and let him play mayor?"

"I *am* the mayor," John insisted with a huff, regaining some of his spirit.

Carter grinned. "Then I suggest you make the most of it and order people around for the rest of the day."

"I'll see he takes it easy." Karen took him

by his good arm. "Carter, just throw his shirt in the trash. I believe it's beyond repair."

"Will do. Sorry about that." Carter picked up the discarded clothing and stuffed it in the garbage can.

"I understand." She and John headed down the hallway and out the front door.

Carter leaned his hip against the counter, crossed his arms over his chest and studied Liz. "Well, you were certainly something, Dr. Poole."

Liz's heart thumped hard under his appraisal. She busied herself with emptying the old ice pack. Was that a compliment or a complaint? Sometimes her social cues could be off.

"I now understand why you're such a valuable member of the medical team at community events."

She looked at him. "Thank you. Who've you been talking to?"

He shrugged. "I asked around about you."

Liz wasn't sure how she felt about that bit of information. "You asked about me?"

"I did."

"Why?" Heat climbed up her neck.

"Because I wanted to know about you. What kind of person you are."

She looked away unable to meet his intense gaze any longer. "Why?"

"Because I like you and I don't trust my judgment where people, women in particular, are concerned, especially after my ex."

"Oh." Her heart jumped into overdrive. That was a forthright answer. One she wasn't prepared for. "It was bad?"

"Yeah. The worst. I can't have someone around Ryan that I can't trust." He took her elbow. "Come on. We'd better get back. All the food'll be gone or cold. Ryan'll be wondering where we are, as well."

Carter hoped he hadn't said anything wrong. Liz had looked both terrified and shocked at his blunt admission. She fascinated him. Tall, sleek and poised, he found her outwardly attractive but even more he liked her willingness to help others. The way she rushed to aid John, reassuring him. Carter hadn't seen a moment of hesitation. Liz knew her medicine and it was obviously the area where she felt comfortable. She had a great bedside manner, as well. Refreshing after his ex-wife's concern only for herself and her needs.

He was glad Liz had decided to come today.

They walked across the green toward the tables where many of his neighbors were already seated, eating.

"This is really an interesting place," Liz said, looking around.

"I didn't have to think twice about buying my grandparents' house when they offered it to me. Ryan and I moved here to lead a peaceful life. Mooresville has given us that. And friends."

"I'm glad you both are happy."

He glanced at her as they continued to walk. Was she happy? Something in her voice made him wonder.

As they reach the group, they received a standing ovation. He grinned and waved everyone down. Liz smiled shyly as if she didn't like the attention.

Carter took her elbow. "Come this way and we'll get some food."

A bright red spot rested on each of her cheeks. She'd been embarrassed by the response. "See, I'm not the only one who thought you did good."

"I was doing what I've been trained to do. No big deal."

"Maybe so, but you were great with John."

As they filled their plates at the long tables covered with food, more than one person said thank-you to them. They moved away from the food tables and Carter said, "Ryan should be sitting with the Wilsons. I saw them down this way."

He noticed her looking at his plate piled high with food. "I don't eat like this every day."

Liz gave him a knowing grin. "If you say so."

Was she teasing him? "You sound like you don't believe me."

Her grin grew to a smile. "I didn't say that."

"Are you concerned as a citizen or as a doctor?" He flirted with her and she was returning it.

Giving him a noncommittal lift of her chin, she said, "Just making an observation."

"That I might need to watch my weight?" He pushed for the back-and-forth to continue.

"Hey, I didn't say that. You know you don't. You look great." Liz's eyes widened before she shook her head and looked away.

Unable to contain it, he barked a laugh. "Why thank you for the compliment, Liz." When she looked at him, he added, "I'm teasing, you know?"

She looked perplexed. "People don't usually tease me."

"I'm glad. That makes me special. I get to see what few do—your beautiful blush."

"Now you're just trying to get me to blush more."

"There's Ryan." Carter continued to the end of a table and put his plate down in front of the chair beside his son's. "Liz, this one's yours." He indicated the place on the other side of him. "I'll go get us something to drink. Is iced tea fine with you or would you like something else?"

"Tea is good."

"Ryan, introduce Liz to Mr. and Mrs. Wilson while I'm gone, will you?"

Carter stepped away for a couple of minutes and returned with two plastic disposable cups. He placed one at his plate and another at hers. As he sat, he said, "Mrs. Wilson, I hope this is your mac and cheese."

His leg brushed along Liz's as he settled into his seat. Heat rushed up and down his leg. He stumbled over the words, but he got them out. "She makes the best."

Liz gave him a concerned look. "She does? I'm glad I got some."

Carter watched as Liz forked into the cheesy noodles. She closed her eyes and savored the taste. The expression on her face made his groin tighten. He forced himself to swallow. What would it be like to have her react to him with such obvious pleasure?

Where had that notion come from? He'd left a horrible relationship. He wasn't looking for anything but friendship. Liz didn't strike him as being someone who'd only be looking for a fling. That's the best he could offer. He and Ryan had finally settled into a good steady life. Rocking what they had wasn't his plan. Yet, the thought of touching, kissing Liz had its appeal. Pulled at him.

A few moments later, Liz said, "Mrs. Wilson, the mac and cheese truly is wonderful. Best I've ever eaten."

"Thank you. And you were impressive in your quick action to help John. I'm sure the burn would've been worse if not for you."

"I just did what needed to be done." Liz made it sound like it was no big deal to her.

"Dad, I can't cut this sausage," Ryan whined, drawing Carter's attention away from Liz.

Carter turned to him. "Let me help."

In the small space, his hip shifted into Liz's thigh. She stiffened against him. Apparently, she felt some of what he did. His body went into sensory overload. Soon he returned to his original position, but the awareness of their closeness didn't disappear.

Over the next few minutes, he made conversation with the Wilsons, all the while too conscious of Liz beside him. Occasionally she joined in with a thoughtful remark.

"Ryan, we're going to need to finish up here," Carter announced.

Liz moved to get up. "I guess I should be going."

Carter turned to her, putting his hand over hers. Hers was cold and he wanted to pull her to him and warm her up. That crazy thought made him pause. Liz had him thinking things he hadn't in a long time. He'd been out with a number of women since his divorce but none that affected him the way Liz did.

"Please don't go. We're just getting started with the festivities. Ryan and I have a surprise for you. We just need to change clothes. We won't be long."

An unsure looked entered her eyes but she nodded.

"Carter didn't tell you?" Mrs. Wilson's look went from him to her. "He's playing the founder of Mooresville, Robert Moore, tonight. Ryan's playing his young son."

"He is?" Liz's attention focused on Carter.

He straightened his shoulders. "You had no idea how important of a man I was, did you?"

Liz's eyes twinkled as she looked at him. "I did not."

"Come on, Ryan. We need to go get dressed." He stood and started cleaning up the plates.

Liz waved his hands away. "Leave those. I'll take care of them since you're such an important person."

Carter grinned. "Thank you. We won't be gone long. I'm sure Mrs. Wilson will keep you company. See you in a few."

CHAPTER THREE

LIZ STOOD AND started gathering the leftover disposable plates and utensils.

"Leave those for a few minutes and let's get to know each other without the men interrupting us," Mrs. Wilson suggested.

Mr. Wilson had left them just before Carter and Ryan had walked away.

What was the older woman after? Liz met her look to find warmth and curiosity in her eyes. Liz's anxiety eased. She lowered herself into the chair.

"I don't know if Carter told you, but Leroy, Mr. Wilson, and I are Carter's grandparents' best friends and Carter's our closest neighbor."

"No, he didn't." Liz wasn't sure where this was going. She feared Mrs. Wilson thought there might be more between Liz and Carter than there was. Or was the older woman going to try to warn Liz off? Which Liz found laughable. She certainly wouldn't consider herself a threat.

"We still stay in touch. So, tell me, how did you and Carter meet?" Mrs. Wilson asked.

"At the community thank-you banquet earlier in the week. He helped me when I had car trouble."

The older woman grinned. "A cute meet. Damsel in distress. Just like in the romances."

Liz stopped a groaned from escaping. She'd not thought of it like that.

"He's a really good father." Mrs. Wilson looked in the direction Carter went. "Devoted to Ryan. Sometimes too much so if you ask me."

Liz turned to watch the man and his son walking tall and proud toward their home.

"Carter's trying hard to be both mother and father to the boy. We've heard horror stories about Ryan's mother."

"Now, Mary, that's enough." Mr. Wilson came up behind his wife and patted her on the shoulder. "Carter might not want you to be telling tales."

Liz cleared her throat and stood, uncomfortable with talking about Carter when he wasn't there. "Carter just invited me here to give him an opinion on the program, whatever that is. We're just friends."

"Those looks he's been giving you say otherwise," Mrs. Wilson murmured.

"I'd better get this cleaned up." Liz placed a used disposable plate on top of another.

With plates in hand, she took them to the nearest large garbage bag. A number of people spoke to her on her way to and from it. She returned to Mr. and Mrs. Wilson. She offered to take their trash and made another trip to the garbage can. On her return, she saw Carter and Ryan coming her way.

Her breath caught. She couldn't help but grin. Maybe there was something to what Mrs. Wilson had implied existed between them. Carter looked so male. He wore a white shirt, long gray vest and navy coat that fit snugly over his wide shoulders. Dark gray flannel pants cuffed just below his knees and white hose molded to his calves with buckled shoes on his feet finished his costume. Carter looked the part of a country gentleman of the 1800s to perfection.

Ryan could have been his twin with the exception he wore no coat. Instead he had a leather vest that tied at his chest. The pair were impressive. Especially the father.

Mrs. Wilson said, "Look how handsome you two are."

Liz lowered her gaze, not wanting Carter to see how much she agreed.

"I'm having problems with this neck cloth." Carter pulled at it. "I can't seem to get it wrapped around my neck right."

"Liz, why don't you help him with that?" Mrs. Wilson suggested.

Was the older woman matchmaking? Unable to gracefully say no, Liz stepped toward Carter.

"I promise not to bite," he whispered.

Her gaze met his. "I'm not afraid."

"Could have fooled me. You've the look of a rabbit ready to jump." Carter's breath flowed across her temple.

Liz shivered. Her hands shook as she took the ends of the neck cloth. "This needs to go around one more time."

Carter stood still as she reached around his neck. He smelled of smoke and something citrusy. His hair brushed the top of her hand. The texture fine and soft. Glad to have her fingers busy, Liz didn't act on her need to caress it just for the pleasure.

She returned to the front of Carter's neck with the material. His look locked with hers. Awareness flickered there. Her center reacted with a jolt. They stood there, looking at each other until the sound of someone clearing their throat caught her attention. Liz refocused on the simple knot she formed. Not soon enough to stop her hands from shaking did she pull the ends out, leaving them to stand straight across his neck. "Mmm…there you go."

"Thank you." Her eyes lifted. They sparkled. "You're ready to dazzle." She turned to Ryan who she felt much more comfortable talking to and bowed slightly. "You look very handsome, young squire."

He turned up his nose and pulled at his clothing. "I don't like this shirt."

Carter put his hand on Ryan's shoulder. "You don't have to wear it forever."

"I hope the other boys don't make fun of me," Ryan whined.

Liz went down on a knee so that she came to his eye level. "I'll tell you a secret." The boy stepped forward, obviously interested. "If they do, it's only because they're jealous that they don't have a part like you do."

"You really think so?" The boy looked at her eagerly.

"I do. People used to make fun of me. It took me a long time, but I learned they were just jealous of what I could do that they couldn't."

"Really?"

"Really."

With a smile, he looked up at Carter. "Okay, Dad. I'm ready."

Over the boy's head Carter mouthed, *Thank you.*

A woman hurried up to them. "Carter, Pam can't be Mrs. Moore. She's stuck in traffic on the bridge. There's been an accident."

Carter groaned. "I guess we'll just have to do it without her."

"Can't someone else be her? Is her dress at her house?" Mrs. Wilson asked.

"It should be. Richard's over there." The woman who had run up pointed.

"Then why can't Liz do it? She and Pam are about the same size. The dress may be a few inches too short but that won't matter." Mrs. Wilson gave her an expectant look.

Liz's eyes went wide as her chest tightened, and she shook her head. Her world was the background. Never up front. "I don't think—"

"You'd be prefect." Carter obviously liked the plan. "Will you do it?"

"I don't know what to do."

"All you have to do is stand beside me. Will you do it?"

How could she turn him down? "Okay."

Carter gave her a quick hug. "Great."

Liz wished it could last longer.

Carter raised an arm and waved. "Richard, come here a sec."

A man with dark hair hurried to them. "Liz has agreed to play Pam's part. Can we get her outfit from you?"

"Sure."

"Ryan," Carter said, "you stay with Mrs. Wilson. We'll be right back."

She and Carter followed the man to a house on the other side of the square. Fifteen minutes later, Liz found herself dressed in a ticking striped dress and wearing a shawl and bonnet. When she stepped into the room where Carter waited, his eyes lit up.

"You look perfect. You'll make an excellent Mrs. Moore."

Liz shook her head. "I don't know about that. I'm not use to being in front of people." That had always been Louisa's role.

"You'll be great." Carter grinned and took her hand. "Then come on, Mrs. Moore. Our audience awaits."

"I could have done without you saying that."

Carter chuckled. "You aren't as big a ham as I am."

Liz walked with him across the square. Maybe she'd just never had a chance to find that out.

When they joined the others, everyone told her she looked great.

Carter studied her and Ryan. "Ready?"

She and Ryan nodded.

Mrs. Wilson smiled. "I, for one, am ready to hear all about Mooresville's history from the lovely Moore family. Y'all look good together."

Mrs. Wilson didn't help her nerves with her implication.

Mr. Wilson spoke to his wife with a warning tone, "Jeanie."

"We'd better get started before the sun sets." Carter winked at Liz, sending a shiver of heat up her spine before he took her hand and they walked over to stand in front of the post office.

"Hello, everyone. Welcome to Mooresville's Christmas Stroll and Caroling." Carter's voice filled the air and drew people's attention.

Liz took her position beside him, trying not to look terrified or shake so much it showed. The crowd circled them.

"I'm Robert Moore and this is my wife, Martha, and our young son, Eli. My brother, William, and I settled here near the Tennessee River in the early 1800s. We were cotton farmers and we found this area perfect for the crop. I hope you're ready to go back in time."

Liz looked around the crowd that had grown

from just those who had shared the meal to a much larger group. Carter had been right. More people had come for the evening. He had them all enthralled in his story. He played the part perfectly. Even she forgot her fear as she got caught up in his words and voice.

As Carter spoke, a couple of photographers' cameras flashed. That didn't seem to faze him. They were as different as winter from summer. Where Carter didn't mind the limelight, she'd have been happy being in the crowd.

Carter continued, "As the years went by, Mooresville grew."

Two women and three men dressed in period costumes joined the three of them.

"Along with homes, we built the post office." Carter pointed toward it. "The Stagecoach Inn for travelers passing through." He took her hand, which was warm and reassuring, and led them through the crowd. Ryan and the other members of the party followed.

He stopped in front of the one-story wooden building with a porch and picket fence around the yard. A wreath of greenery and apples hung on the gate, another on the door. That opened and out stepped a man and woman dressed in period outfits. They joined Carter. He turned and faced the people and post office again.

"From here you can see the sign above the door of the post office indicating that Mooresville became an official town in 1818. It's the oldest town in Alabama. My brother and I along with the other families living here partitioned to become an incorporated township while Alabama was still just a territory. On November sixteenth, 1818, we became official. Today our entire town is on the National Register of Historic Places.

"Now if you'll follow me." His little band of enactors along with Liz firmly in hand and the crowd went with him.

Carter was completely in his element. She, along with the others, remained enthralled with his telling of the story of Mooresville.

They strolled to the end of the next square to where a white clapboard church with a tall steeple stood. Carter stopped in front of it and everyone else did, as well. She noticed that the crowd had grown.

Ryan came to stand in front of them. He started to fidget and she took his hand. The boy settled. Carter gave her a slight smile and went back to what he had been saying.

"By the time we became a township, we were large enough to have two churches. This is the Church of Christ." Carter paused for effect. "Here President James A. Garfield once preached."

Another couple with a teenage girl who were dressed up joined the group.

"We've one more stop." Carter looked at her and grinned.

A warmth filled Liz from the inside out.

"The place where Mrs. Moore and I were married."

Heat washed over her. Liz was grateful for the waning light so that her blush didn't show.

The group continued up the opposite side of the square. As they passed a house, the Wilsons came out the front door dressed in their 1800s clothes and blended in with their neighbors. From there, Carter started across the square toward the large redbrick building with two white columns. The lights were burning and the doors stood open.

Others, including John and Karen stood on the portico waiting. They too were in costume. John still held the peas on his arm.

Carter left her and Ryan in the grass in front of the church. He stepped under the porch in the center of the doors. He turned to face the group. The light glowed behind him, making him more impressive. "This is the Brick Church and the last of the four original buildings in Mooresville. The historic buildings are maintained by those of us who live here in order to preserve the history of our town. Mooresville is often called Alabama's Williamsburg.

"We invite you to join us in singing Christmas carols and having wassail afterward. I speak for all of us who live in Mooresville. We wish you all the best of holiday seasons. Thank you for joining us tonight."

Everyone clapped.

Carter reached his hands out to her and Ryan. They each placed theirs in his. His fingers clasped her cool ones, blanketing them in warmth. Together they entered the church. He led them down the center to a front row. There they sat. To her astonishment, Carter continued to hold her hand and even more surprisingly, she allowed it.

Only when Mrs. Wilson handed them a booklet filled with Christmas carols did he release her hand. She missed his touch deeply. The song "O Holy Night" was announced and Carter turned the pages until he found it. He had a beautiful voice. She'd always loved to sing, but her mother had told her long ago her voice wasn't as nice as Louisa's, so Liz didn't sing much in public.

Carter leaned over and whispered, "You can do better than that."

On the next song, she sang more freely. By the time they were done, she no longer cared who heard her. She'd enjoyed the music. In the high-ceilinged sanctuary, the sound of joined voices without accompaniment had been magical. They ended with "We Wish You a Merry Christmas." It was a Christmas experience she'd always treasure.

Afterward Carter asked her, "Would you like to have something to drink?"

"I probably should be going."

"Daddy, I want to change clothes." Ryan circled his father.

"Okay. You were extra good tonight." Carter mussed his hair. "Thanks for playing your part so well." His eyes met hers. "You were wonderful, as well. Thanks for helping out."

"Not a problem." To Ryan she said, "I agree with your dad. You were great." She looked at Carter. "You were, as well. That was a wonderful presentation. I was impressed."

Carter straightened his shoulders, puffed out his chest and looked down his nose at her. "You sound like you hadn't expected I had theatrics in me."

"I never implied that." He was teasing her again. "I also loved the way people dressed up and kept joining the group."

"Thanks. We in Mooresville take our history seriously."

She smiled. "I can see that. I liked being a part of it." To her surprise, she had. She'd certainly stepped out of her comfort zone today. In more ways than one.

"I'm glad you did." Carter pulled on his neck cloth. "Come on. I think we've had enough of the past for today."

The sun had set while they were inside. Carter walked with confidence across the yard toward his house. On unfamiliar ground, Liz stumbled. Carter's hand came to her waist to steady her. He took her hand and placed it around his arm.

"Hold on. I know where to step and not to. I don't want you falling headfirst."

Liz lightly touched his arm, then the ground dipped again, and she gripped it until they reached the pavement.

"Don't let go here either. Some of this road is pretty old." Carter's smooth voice reassured her in the darkness.

Ryan ran ahead of them, just visible in the moonlight.

"Straight to the house," Carter called to him. He said to her, "I'm glad we blocked off the street from the main road. I don't have to worry about him getting hit."

"I need to get my clothes and change. Return this dress." Liz pulled away.

Carter tugged her back. "I asked Richard to put them in a bag and leave them on my porch. You can change at my place. I'll return the dress."

By now the lights of homes and buildings were coming on. The homes had single candles in the windows. It was like being back in a slower, easier time. "This place truly is wonderful."

"I thought you might enjoy tonight." His voice came through the dark, deep and rich, soothing.

"Why did you think that?"

"Because you looked around when you came to my house the other night like a kid does when they get a gift they've been wanting."

How could he read her so well? They hardly knew each other.

"I do like old buildings and history. Thanks for inviting me to eat also. Oh, man, I forgot my pie plate." She moved to let go of his arm.

His hand came over hers, stopping her. "Don't worry about it. Someone will take it home, clean it and it'll turn up on my doorstep. I'll see you get it back. Dang, I didn't get a piece of your pie. I hate that." He gave her a pleading look. "Is there any way I might get some another day?"

She liked the tingle that went through her at the idea of Carter wanting to see her again. "You don't even know if it was any good."

"I figure that if you brought it, then you thought it was your best."

It was her go-to recipe. "Do you enjoy always knowing what I'm thinking?"

He felt more than saw him shrug. "I didn't know I did. Interesting. I might be able to use that to my advantage."

Wednesday morning Carter looked at his watch. He was actually ahead of schedule seeing patients. That almost never happened. On an impulse he picked up his phone. He'd use the extra time to have lunch with Liz. If she'd agree.

He'd thought about her far too often over the last few days. She'd been welcome company at the Christmas event. He'd been impressed she'd joined in as Pam's replacement. One thing he'd learned in the short amount of time he'd known Liz was that she liked to help out others. She'd been quick to care for John, then willing to help with the Stroll and had even put Ryan at ease when he'd been afraid of being made fun of. Something about how she'd told that anecdote made him wonder about her childhood.

Whatever had happened then apparently was no longer an issue because she fit in well with his friends. Almost too much so. Mrs. Wilson obviously liked Liz. She'd told him the other day when he'd been out in the yard he should start dating. She'd even offered to babysit Ryan. Carter liked being around Liz, found her stimulating. Yet he didn't know if he could trust his instincts where women were concerned. His ex-wife had certainly proved his inability to do so. He couldn't afford to make a mistake again.

After his marriage he'd sworn not to take any more chances no matter how much he liked the woman. He had Ryan's welfare to consider. Carter couldn't let him down. Trust was difficult for him to give, especially after it had been thrown back in his face. Carter shook his head. All that was overthinking. He intended just to ask Liz out to a friendly lunch. He was *not* offering marriage.

Liz's receptionist answered the phone. While he waited for Liz to come on the line, he drummed a finger against his desk. Why did it matter to him so much whether she agreed to meet him or not? If she said no, it wouldn't be a big deal. Yet he really wanted to see her.

"This is Dr. Poole."

"This is Dr. Jacobs." He mimicked her tone.

"Hi, Carter."

He smiled. Her words were low and shy-sounding. Was she as unsure about him as he was of her? "I'm calling to see if you'd like to meet me for lunch at a café on Sixth. That's about halfway between our offices."

"If I do, I have to be back to see patients by one thirty."

He used his most encouraging tone. "They're fast at the café. I promise to have you home by curfew time."

"Funny. Very funny."

Carter chuckled.

"I usually just eat here, but I'll make an exception this time. I think I'd like to get out today."

She made it sound as if he were a good excuse to do something she wanted to do anyway. Carter wasn't sure he liked that. All of a sudden he really hoped she wanted to see *him*. "Good."

"I can meet you in thirty minutes."

Why did his heart beat faster? It was just lunch. "Great. I'll see you at Café Decatur. Do you know the place?"

"I do."

"See you in a few, Liz." With a grin on his face, he hung up.

Carter stood just outside the café door while he watched Liz step out of her car. She had great legs. Today she wore a dress with a coat over it and tall black boots. Those legs of hers made him think thoughts that had nothing to do with friendship.

Shaking his head to clear those erotic ideas, he smiled and waved. "Hey."

"Hi." She gave him a timid smile.

Carter held the door for her to enter. "There's an open table over here." He led her to it. It sat next to the wall but where they could see out a window.

Before they could say more, the waitress joined them. "Hello, Dr. Jacobs. How're you today?"

He grinned at the girl who regularly waited on him. "Fine, Lucy. You?"

She cocked a hip and give him a come-on smile. He'd seen it so often he didn't take it seriously. "Doing great. What can I get you? Your usual?"

Carter glanced at Liz, who watched their exchange with interest. "Yes, but first see what Dr. Poole would like."

Liz picked up the menu that had been stuck between the napkin dispenser and the salt and pepper shakers. "Uh…how about the…green salad with chicken and an iced tea."

The girl wrote it down. "Will do."

As soon as she'd left, Liz met his gaze with brows raised. "Come here often?"

He shrugged. "A couple of times a week. I like to get out of the office. I usually walk over so I can get the free exercise and some fresh air."

"And apparently you've got a regular waitress." She fiddled with the saltshaker.

"Well, maybe I do tend to sit at the same table." He grinned at her.

Her eyes narrowed. "Your usual would be?"

Carter didn't hesitate. "Ham and cheese on rye, potato chips and an iced tea."

"Sounds good."

He liked that she had relaxed some. Crossing his arms on the table, he leaned toward her. "So, how have you been?"

"Fine."

"I'm glad you came Saturday. Must've been a bit overwhelming. Especially when you were pulled into the program. I hadn't intended to do that to you."

"I have to admit, I'm not used to being in front of people, but I did enjoy the program."

She'd said the same thing Saturday as she'd left, but his ex-wife had lied to him so often he wasn't sure if he could recognize the truth anymore.

"How's John doing?"

"The burn is healing. I changed the bandage."

She nodded and placed her hands in her lap as if she'd realized she'd been abusing the shaker. "Good."

He grinned. "It seems like every time we're together there's some kind of excitement."

Liz looked over her shoulder toward the kitchen. "Should we say something to the people back there about being extra careful?"

A bang of pans falling filled the air. Their looks met a few seconds before they broke out in laughter. They couldn't stop. Carter glanced around to see other customers staring at them. Still he continued to chuckle.

Liz mesmerized him in her mirth. It changed her appearance from attractive to beautiful. If he hadn't found her interesting before, he certainly did now.

"We have to stop," she gasped. "People are looking at us."

Carter chuckled. "I can't if you keep laughing."

"Okay, on three we stop. One, two, three." She gulped for air on the last word.

Carter had to look away not to start laughing again. Thankfully their waitress brought their drinks and they sobered up.

Liz leaned toward him, still smiling. "If we aren't careful, we're going to be asked to leave."

"It'd be worth it. I needed a good laugh. I don't do that often enough. I've had a few lean years where laughter is concerned."

"Come to think of it, laughter is supposed to be the best medicine." Liz grinned.

He pointed a finger at her. "Don't you get us started again."

"That's funny." She quickly closed her mouth and looked away.

He took a swallow of his tea. "What's that look for?"

"I was thinking how ironic it is that I've been told I act like a wallflower and now you're accusing me of creating a scene."

"I didn't exactly say that." He grinned. Had she always stood in the background? Why?

Her eyelids flickered up, then down. "That's what I heard."

"Let's examine the evidence. I've seen you three times and you've had car trouble, taken care of a burned arm and pots have fallen.

There's nothing quiet and unassuming about any of that. I don't know who's been lying to you or if you've been hiding all that talent on purpose but I've had more excitement in my life in the last few days than I've had in months because of you."

Liz lifted her head, her eyes bright. "Really?"

"Yeah, really."

"Me, exciting." She spoke more to herself than to him, amazement in her voice. A grin slowly formed on her lips.

He smiled as their food arrived.

"You're working the flotilla during the Festival of Trees on the River this weekend, aren't you?" Carter asked before taking a bite of his sandwich.

"I am."

"I'm surprised you're an ENT when you're so good with emergency work." He watched her as she pushed around a cucumber.

Her gaze flickered up to his. "My sister wanted us to be ENTs. She wasn't wild about blood."

He huffed. "But she's a doctor? So, you're partners with your sister? Interesting."

Liz put down her fork and placed her hands in her lap. "Not any more. She died, August a year ago."

This he hadn't expected. He shook his head. "I'm so sorry to hear that."

"She was my twin sister."

Carter felt a stabbing pain in his chest for what Liz had suffered. To lose a sister was bad enough, but a twin sister made it worse. "Liz, I..."

"I know. I usually don't tell anyone because they have the same reaction. I not only lost my sister but my best friend and medical partner."

"I'd like to know about her if you want to talk about her?"

"Louisa and I weren't identical twins. We had some similarities in looks but just those of average sisters. Our personalities were our biggest difference. She was far more outgoing than me. Everyone loved her." Liz let the words trail off. "Do you have any brothers or sisters?"

Liz obviously didn't want to talk about her sister anymore. "I have a brother. He and his wife live overseas. He's in the military."

"So you don't get to see them often."

"I don't but when I do, it's like slipping back to where we were. We have a great time together."

She gave him a weak smile. "That's nice. Do your mother and father live close?"

"They live about three hours away." He took a bite of his sandwich.

"It's nice they don't live too far away. Ryan can see them often."

But that wasn't the case. Carter made excuses for them not to visit. When they were around, it just reminded him of how poorly his marriage had gone. What a disappointment to them and himself he'd been. His parents had the perfect marriage. They'd been married for thirty-eight years and he couldn't even make one last three years. They reminded him every time he saw them of his failure. His mistake.

"We don't see them as much as they or Ryan would like."

"Not you?"

"Me too. Of course," he quickly added.

She studied him a moment longer than made him comfortable. She wiped her mouth with her napkin. "I really should be getting back. I've a full list of patients this afternoon."

"Hold on a sec. I'll walk you out." Carter took one more swallow of his drink and picked up the check the waitress had left.

Liz led the way to the cash register. "I'll get mine." She reached for the check.

"I'll take care of it. You can get it next time if you want."

Liz waited near the door while he paid.

She acted eager to leave. Their light lunch had turned heavier than he'd planned. Talking about her sister had rattled them both. He thought he knew hurt but his couldn't have been anywhere near hers.

"Hey—" he took her hand before she ran to the car "—I enjoyed seeing you again. Let's do it again sometime."

She finally looked at him. "Okay."

"In fact, why don't we do it Friday night?"

Liz gave him a wry smile. "That's not lunchtime and I already have plans. I'm working the Festival of Trees, remember?"

He slapped his thigh. "That's right, I forgot. We'll try another time. I'll call you. Bye, Liz." He kissed her cheek. As he watched her walk away, he grinned as her hand came to rest over the spot where his lips had been.

CHAPTER FOUR

LIZ LOOKED OUT of the medical tent at the crowd lining the river in front of her. The sun had almost set, and the Festival of Trees on the River had drawn a large mob this year with the weather having turned clear and crisp. Perfect for bundling up, hot chocolate and floating boats.

She and her EMT help, Ricky, had cared for a few patients in the last hour: a young boy with a nosebleed; after him came a girl who had fallen and needed her hands cleaned and bandaged; a woman who had been hit in the head when a boy threw a rock. The list, thankfully only filled with small problems, kept growing.

On her way to retrieve additional gauze from the supply box, she glanced up to see Carter and Ryan standing close by.

"Hi." Carter smiled. "We came by to say hello. How're things going?"

"Steady, nothing major. Hey there, Ryan. Are you ready for the parade?"

The boy nodded. "I've never seen a boat parade."

"I promise you'll like this one. My sister and I used to beg to come every year." Why had she said that? She hadn't thought of those days in a long time. To her surprise, remembering felt good. It seemed easier to say now that Carter knew about Louisa. Their lunch had had some difficult emotional moments for her but after she'd talked about Louisa she felt better. She needed to do that more often.

In the distance Christmas music began to fill the air.

"Come on, Dad." Ryan pulled on Carter's hand. "It's starting. We've got to go. My friend Mike's already down there."

"Better go. Come join us if you get a chance," Carter said over his shoulder, as Ryan pulled him away.

"Thanks. I'll see." Liz returned his smile, although she doubted she'd make it. Being responsible, she couldn't leave the tent. Disappointment filled her as she watched Carter and Ryan. She moved to the front of the tent but could no longer see them. She liked Carter. He had quickly become a friend. The fact he was a handsome eligible male didn't hurt. It had been a long time since she'd felt about a man the way she did about Carter.

Liz's attention became diverted by a man coming up with his hand wrapped in a bloody rag. He'd been using a pocketknife and it had slipped. The result ended up being an ugly gash in his palm. She and Ricky were just finishing up with him when a teenager came running toward them from the direction of the river.

"Help! Help! We need some help."

Liz rushed out to meet him. "What's wrong?"

The guy pointed back behind him. "A man on a boat got his arm caught."

"Listen! Go tell them not to move him until I get there! Tell them not to move him," Liz repeated. "I'm on my way."

She turned and Ricky handed her the go-bag. "Stay on the radio. I'll call if I need you."

"Ten-four."

Slinging her bag over her shoulder, Liz took off running. She soon caught up with the teen. The crowd parted.

A low-in-the-water fishing boat was parked parallel to the bank and held there by two men with ropes. The craft had been decorated with bright Christmas lights and had a tree standing in the middle with more lights strung from the top of the tree to the corners of the boat. There were more bulbs lining the edge. Children dressed as angels sat and stood in the boat.

As she reached the river's edge, her breath caught and her heart pounded. What caught her attention could only be the worst sight she'd ever seen. A man lay half on and half off the back of the boat. A woman supported his head and had it turned to the side so his face remained out of the water. His right arm appeared pinned under the motor.

Two men started to raise the motor.

"Stop! Don't do that!" she yelled.

The men turned with obvious surprise.

She stepped over the side of the boat, careful not to make it rock. "I'm Dr. Poole. We don't want him to bleed out in case the radial artery has been severed. The pressure of the motor may keep him from losing his life or his arm."

Slowly she moved closer to the back of the boat. When it sank deeper in the water, she stopped.

"We're going to need to get some ballast to the front," a voice Liz recognized came from behind her. She glanced over her shoulder to see Carter standing toward the front. He didn't wait on her agreement before he said, "I'm

Dr. Jacobs. I need all the children to get off the boat."

He pointed to two women. "You and you—help them off and stay with them until their parents get here. Everyone else, move to the front as far as you can." He pointed. "Including you two gentlemen in the back. Dr. Poole and I'll call you back when we're ready for you to lift the motor."

Liz wasted no time moving to the patient as the weight shifted, bringing the back of the boat farther out of the water. She went down on her knees beside the man and took over the lady's job of keeping his head out of the water. Liz gently cupped his cheek so that she could turn his face toward her. In the dim light, she could easily see the man's skin color had turned white. His eyes were wide and pupils large. He was going into shock. Liz feared he might pass out.

A strong light blinked on. She glanced back to see Carter, with his legs wide to steady himself on the floor of the boat, pointing a large flashlight in her direction.

She took a second look at the man's arm. It lay between the bottom of the large outboard motor and the top of the transom of the boat. She winced. He'd have a tough time keeping his arm. It looked crushed.

"Carter, I need some blankets or coats. He's going into shock."

He nodded and stepped to the front and spoke to the people.

"Can you move your fingers?" she asked the injured man, keeping her voice even despite the pace of her heart.

"Yes," he grunted.

"Good." That at least was encouraging. "We're going to get this motor off you and you to the hospital as soon as we can. Carter," she spoke over her shoulder, "I'm going to need you back here with me. We'll need those men now."

"Give me a sec to do some more counterbalancing. Both of us needing to be in the same corner of the boat is going to be problematic."

The light disappeared but soon returned. She looked back to find a man turned around on his knees in the driver's seat, holding the flashlight high. Liz returned her attention to the injured man while Carter went about trying to make them as safe as possible. "Can you tell me what happened?"

"Something got caught in the motor," her patient replied through clenched teeth. "I pulled to the bank and raised the motor. I reached under it, but the hydraulic lift gave out. The motor came down on my arm before I could pull it out." As he spoke, his voice became more labored.

She looked away from him to see Carter directing men to the other side of the boat while guiding two more to stand near the motor. He lay a blanket, then a couple of heavy coats over the man's body.

"I've disengaged the gear. We're ready when you are," Carter said.

"I'm going to need you down here with me. In my bag you'll find a splint and a package of eight-by-eight absorbent squares. Open a couple of those and have more on standby."

Carter worked quickly, soon coming to stand beside her. The back corner of the boat dipped low in the water. A trickle of liquid wet her side. Half the man's face lay in the freezing water.

Carter spoke to the two men, "As soon as you have the motor up and secure, I want you to move toward the front of the boat."

Both nodded.

Liz did her best to keep her teeth from chattering. "Carter, I'm going to need to support the arm and you to apply pressure as soon as you can. I'll pull him back and keep his head out of the water. We all go on three. One, two, three."

With low grunts, the men lifted the motor.

Liz scooted and pulled the hurt man back against her body with one arm across his torso, holding up his head the best she could. She realized the moment the man passed out because he went limp and his head became heavier. Pulling hard, she held his back against her chest to keep him from drowning.

Over the injured man's shoulder, she watched as Carter positioned the splint and applied the large pads to the blood pouring from the wound on the top of his forearm. Liz put two fingers to his neck and located his carotid artery. "His pulse is low."

"I'm not surprised. He's lost a lot of blood. Would've lost more if they had lifted the motor. You were smart to stop them. Good work."

His praised warmed her despite the cold water running down her back.

"I'll get you out from under him just as soon as I get this arm secured," Carter promised. He called, "I need someone light in weight to help me with a bandage."

A woman joined him, going through the bag and finding a roll of elastic bandage.

"Start above his elbow and wrap but not too tightly," Carter instructed.

The woman started to work.

"You okay down there, Liz?" Carter asked.

"Yeah." Despite the fact she had a heavy man lying over her and her cheek and neck were smashed against the boat. There would be a mark for a while, but her discomfort came nowhere to matching her patient's. She shivered as more water rolled down her back. Truthfully she'd be more than happy to get up. "We need an ambulance."

"Already on the way. I radioed Ricky before we pulled the motor up." Carter's attention remained focused on the woman's work. "That's good. You're doing a great job."

His tone offered the obviously nervous woman encouragement. Liz liked Carter's ability to anticipate needs during an emergency and to make people feel at ease. That talent was a special one.

He gave the woman a reassuring smile. "There should be a Velcro end on that. All you have to do is press it down."

She did as Carter instructed.

He smiled at her. "Perfect. You can be my assistant anytime."

The woman returned the smile, indicating Carter had clearly charmed her. He announced, "Liz, now we need to get this man off you."

The boat shifted.

Carter called over his shoulder. "Hey, I need

everyone to stay put until we have this man off the boat. Please stand still." His tone allowed for no argument. "All right, Liz, I'm going to roll him toward me. I want you to shift out from under him. Can you do that?"

"Yeah." It wouldn't be easy, but she'd do it.

"Protect his arm."

"Ten-four. Here we go." Carter slowly rolled the man toward him onto his good shoulder.

Liz pushed against the man's back being careful not to apply any pressure to his bad shoulder. Slowly she shifted out from under him, inhaling in her first full breath in a while. Staying on her knees, she helped Carter lower the man back down to the floor of the boat and adjust the blanket.

Soon the sound of the ambulance arriving filled the air.

Preoccupied, Liz said, "If you'll hand me the bag, I'll get some vitals. Also, that life preserver. Put it under his feet to help with the shock."

Carter handed her the bag, then the life preserver. "If you are okay here, I'll meet the EMTs."

She nodded, then started checking the man's heart rate, blood pressure, for further injuries, then made sure the bandage didn't restrict more blood flow than necessary. All the while she remained aware of Carter working behind her.

A few minutes later, a woman said in a shaky voice, "That man told me to bring this to you."

Liz took a blanket from her. "Thanks."

"Thank you. This is my husband."

Liz stopped long enough to place her hand on the woman's arm. "He's going to be fine. Hang in there. Will you help me put this blanket over him?"

Together they got it into place.

Carter returned with the EMTs who carried a board. She tried to stand but stumbled because her legs were stiff. Carter's hand took her elbow, steadying her, and remained there as they stepped back so the EMTs could work on the rocking boat. He let go only to help the EMTs carry the patient to the ambulance.

Once the patient was inside, she gave a report and soon the ambulance pulled away with its lights on. Liz rolled her shoulders and her teeth chattered.

A blanket came around her shoulders and large hands adjusted it. "You have to be freezing. Your back is soaked. Let's get you back to the tent. See if we can find you something dry and warm."

"Sounds good. I need to check on Ricky." She looked around. "By the way, where's Ryan?"

"With some friends. We were standing with them when I saw you running toward the boat. I figured you might need some help."

"I did. Much appreciated help. I hate that you missed watching the parade with Ryan."

He shrugged. "There's next year."

"You're a nice guy, Carter Jacobs."

He grinned. "Thanks, but it's more like I have a soft spot for you."

Heat washed through her that had nothing to do with the blanket or the blood once again flowing freely in her limbs. "You shouldn't say things like that to me."

"Why not? It's true. Why do you think I wouldn't be interested in you?"

She had a difficult time looking at him. "I guess because through the years most guys have either found me too smart to be fun or weird. My last boyfriend stopped dating me because he said I was dull."

Carter put a hand on her arm and took a step closer, giving her an earnest look. "I assure you, you're not dull. Case in point, the last hour I spent with you. Please don't hide who you are from me. Ever."

What had Liz's ex-boyfriend been thinking to tell her something so untrue? In Carter's experience, she couldn't have been further from being dull. Her intelligence made her interesting. It made their conversations thought-provoking. What he found more fascinating was his reaction to her.

After his ugly marriage and divorce, he'd kept his distance from women. He'd dated occasionally but with little enthusiasm. Something about Liz pulled at him. At first, she'd seemed more like a damsel in need of his help only to morph into super medical woman when she was needed. It made him wonder what facet of her personality he'd discover next. His curiosity had been piqued.

Being around Liz made him question what might happen next. Excitement he'd not known in a long time made him look forward to the next day and the possibility of seeing her. She added an anticipation to his life that Ryan and work alone didn't fill.

"Hey," she said to Ricky, as she entered the tent and dropped her go-bag on the table.

"How did things go?" Ricky asked.

"Patient's gone. I sure hope he gets to keep

his arm." Liz picked up a bottle of water and handed it to Carter before she took one for herself.

Ricky nodded. "Why don't you take a few minutes to regroup? I've got things under control here. The parade isn't over yet. Go catch the last of it."

Liz huffed. "I can't leave you. Who knows what'll happen?"

"You could go straight down from here." Ricky pointed the way out of the tent. "You'd be close enough to come right back. I can text you if I need you."

She grimaced but indecision still rooted her there. "I'd like to see some of the parade." She sounded wistful.

"Then come on." Carter took her hand.

"I need to put on a dry shirt first. Get rid of this blanket."

"Do it, then we'll go." Carter gave her a nudge on her back.

"You'll wait?"

Carter nodded. "I'll wait."

Liz smiled and hurried to a nearby car and grabbed a bag, then scrambled into the side door of the medical van. She soon returned with a heavy sweater on. "Okay. I'm ready." She pointed her finger at Rick. "But you call me if I'm needed."

Carter escorted her to the riverbank and they joined the crowd. She appeared surprised and happy they'd found Ryan and the family he was with. Carter quickly introduced her, but the boats were going by and they had no time to talk. Ryan came to stand between them.

"Hi there, Ryan," Liz said enthusiastically.

"Hey, Miss Liz."

"Have you been having a good time?" Liz's attention remained on his son.

"Uh-huh," Ryan answered.

"I'm glad. This is one of my favorite events. The boat owners are always so creative with their decorations."

Before she could say more "Here Comes Santa Claus" could be heard playing. "Hey, buddy," Carter said to Ryan, "let me put you on my shoulders so you can see."

With his son securely on his shoulders, the crowd pressed in, shifting Carter closer to Liz. His free hand brushed hers. He sought her touch again, intertwining their fingers. Carter glanced at her. "I don't want to lose you."

In an odd way, he meant that on a higher level. That shook him. He didn't even know if he could trust himself to feel that way.

Her gaze met his for a moment before she blinked and once again focused on the boats. Glad she hadn't pulled away, he tightened his grip. She adjusted her hand, applying the same pressure.

Smiling, he returned his attention to the flotilla. A glance at Liz revealed she watched the boats with great interest and with a large smile on her face. Liz didn't need to look for excitement elsewhere like his ex-wife had. She really did enjoy simple pleasures.

When Santa had passed, the crowd dispersed and Carter grinned at her. "That was really neat." He lifted Ryan down. "We're gonna make this an annual event, aren't we, buddy?"

His son eagerly nodded.

Carter casually remarked, "Liz, I should hang out with you more often. There's always something exciting happening."

She grinned and freed her fingers. "I think you might be giving me more credit than you should. I've got to go back to the med tent and help pack it away. I'm glad you came tonight. And thanks for your help. I really appreciated it." Liz turned to go.

Carter grabbed her wrist, stopping her. "Ryan and I are going for pizza. You want to join us?"

She looked back toward the tent. "I don't know how long it'll take me to pack up."

"I'll tell you what, I'll text you what pizza

place we're at when we decide. You can join us if you want. I hope you will."

And he did, very much. He wanted to spend more time with Liz. Have the chance to touch her again. Maybe more.

The entire time Liz hurried to pack away items in the medical tent excitement built in her at the idea of spending more time with Carter. He and Ryan were waiting on her. *Her.* Having a man attracted to her was stimulating. To have it be a handsome, intelligent and fun man like Carter made it even more thrilling. She liked him, too much. She had no doubt hurt lay ahead, but for now she would make the most of the time while it lasted.

Her phone dinged with a text. Carter and Ryan were at Pizza Joe's. It was her favorite pizza place in town.

"Go on. I've got this. I owe you anyway," Ricky said.

"Are you sure?" She had never thought of leaving a colleague like this before.

"I'm sure. Go on." He waved her away.

Liz picked up her purse. "Okay, but call me if you've a problem and I'll come right back."

"I'm good." Ricky returned to packing away a box. "We're almost done here anyway."

With a smile on her face and her blood humming, she climbed into her car and headed to the restaurant. Twenty minutes later she walked in the door of the darkened pizza joint located in a strip mall.

As if she were a heat-seeking missile and Carter the target, she found him immediately. He smiled, motioning her over to his and Ryan's booth. He sat on one side and Ryan on the other bench. Carter slid out and stood, waiting on her.

"Hi, gentlemen. I heard that I could get a good pizza here." What was she doing? That sounded too much like flirting. She didn't flirt. Didn't even know how to.

A quizzical expression came over Ryan's face. "It's a pizza restaurant so they have pizza."

She and Carter laughed. "You're right, and it's the best. My favorite place."

"Ryan said he was a big boy and wanted to sit by himself." Carter indicated with a hand for her to slide in. "So, you'll need to join me."

Liz gave him a speculative look. Had Carter put Ryan up to not sharing his bench so that she had to sit next to him? "Okay." She settled on the bench, placing her purse between her and Carter, making sure they wouldn't touch.

"Why don't you put that over there with

Ryan where it'll be out of the way?" Carter suggested.

Unable to think of a good reason to disagree, she handed the purse to Carter and he placed it on the other bench. So much for her having a line of defense. The second her purse was removed her and Carter's legs met from hip to knee. Warmth simmered along her thigh.

He smiled. "That's better, isn't it?"

She couldn't say it wasn't, so she said nothing. Thankfully moments later the waiter arrived to take their drink order.

Liz grinned at Ryan. "I guess you're going to have cheese pizza."

Ryan bobbed his head.

"I'm having meat lover's," she announced.

Soon the waiter returned with their drinks.

Carter placed their order. As the waiter left, he shifted on the bench and gave her a head-to-toe appraisal. "I don't know where you put all that meat. It certainly doesn't show that I can see."

Liz's face heated. She leaned over the table and spoke to Ryan, "Do you think we should share ours with your dad?"

The boy acted as if he gave it serious thought. "Maybe one piece if we have enough."

"Ryan!" Carter sounded indignant but mirth filled his voice.

Liz put her hand out. "Agreed." She and Ryan shook hands.

Carter huffed and glared at them. "Hey, I didn't plan to be ganged up on when I suggested we go for pizza."

"You're not being ganged up on. We're just greedy where our pizza is concerned. Isn't that right, Ryan?"

He nodded with a grin on his face.

"So, what's the plan? For me to watch you two eat until you're full?" Disbelief circled Carter's words but he grinned.

"Maybe," Liz answered as seriously as possible. She like the banter. There wasn't enough of this type of interaction in her life.

"I think I'd better order my own after all." He raised a hand.

Liz placed hers on his forearm. "We're just kidding you."

"Yeah, Dad," Ryan said. "I'll give you a piece."

"And I will too." Liz added a sweet note to her voice. "We wouldn't want you to go away hungry."

Carter looked into her eyes. His holding a blaze. He said softly, "Maybe I should satisfy my hunger in another way."

Liz's eyes widened. She swallowed hard. Was Carter implying what she thought he was?

Just as quickly his attention returned to his son. "Ryan, did you like the parade?"

He nodded.

Liz watched the child closely as she clutched her shaking hands in her lap. "Which was your favorite?"

"Santa Claus." The boy didn't hesitate.

She chuckled and so did Carter.

"Stepped into that one, didn't you?" Carter nudged her with his shoulder.

She glanced at him and smiled before returning her attention to Ryan. "What was your next favorite?"

"The one with the big blue tree and all the blue lights. The big fish was funny."

Liz nodded. "I know the one you're talking about. It was the one decorated like the catfish was swallowing the tree."

Ryan nodded, grinning.

"That figures." Carter asked her, "What was your favorite?"

"I like them all, but my favorite is always the pink frilly one with water ballerinas."

"Ooh, that's a girl float," Ryan complained.

Liz sat straighter. "If you haven't noticed, I'm a girl."

"I've noticed," Carter said in a tone that caused heat to whip through Liz again as his leg pressed against hers. Her hand trembled as she reached for her water glass, hoping to calm her nerves.

Carter picked up the discussion about the floating parade with Ryan. Liz enjoyed listening to the father–son conversation. Carter was a great parent. Especially so since he did it all on his own. What had happened to ruin his marriage? She couldn't imagine a woman not wanting either one of these males.

"My cheese pizza," Ryan announced, squirming in anticipation as the waiter approached their table, holding large pans.

Liz inhaled the wonderful smell of tomato sauce and meat. Carter handed out the plates that had been left for them. A feeling of rightness fell over her. When was the last time she'd been this carefree or had so much fun? For once she didn't feel like she'd been invited because it was the polite thing to do. Louisa had always asked if Liz could come too. This time she didn't feel like an afterthought.

"What're you asking Santa Claus for this Christmas?" Liz watched Ryan stuff pizza into his mouth.

Ryan said, "I want a puppy,"

Carter laughed. "Ryan's been trying to talk me into a dog for months."

"And how's that going?" she asked Carter.

Before Carter could answer, Ryan said in

a bemoaned tone, "He says we've got to wait to make sure that I'm big enough to take care of a dog."

Liz thought for a moment before saying, "They're a big responsibility. I used to have one. They can be a lot of work but give a lot of love." She and Louisa had shared a poodle as children. It had always wanted to sleep on Liz's bed. Her sister hadn't liked that. Louisa had wanted to be his favorite. Liz hadn't realized that until this moment.

"Hey, are you all right?" Carter asked.

She looked at him and blinked. "Uh, yeah. I'm fine."

"You disappeared for a few moments there."

Liz forced a smile. "I was just thinking how much I've missed having a dog."

"See, Dad? Even Miss Liz thinks I need to get a dog."

Holding up a hand, she said, "Whoa, whoa! Don't put me in the middle of that argument."

Carter chuckled, obviously enjoying the exchange. "Welcome to the world of parenthood. Any slip of the tongue will be used against you."

"You two need to keep me out of it. I think I'll be quiet now." She took a big bite of her pizza.

Carter laughed. "You know I've not had this much fun in a long time."

Come to think of it, neither had she. Liz blinked. This was what happiness felt like.

"Daddy, when're we going to put up the Christmas tree?"

"I guess we better do that this weekend. I'm on call the next." He ate some of his pizza.

"Can it have the big lights with the different colors?" Ryan asked.

Carter wiped his mouth. "I don't know. We don't have any of those. We'd have to buy some."

"I bought some extra last year that I'm not going to use. You're welcome to them." Liz's heart expanded at the excitement on Ryan's face. She looked at Carter. "I can drop them off at your office."

Carter shook his head. "We can't take your lights. You might need them."

"Sure you can. I'm not going to use them," she assured him.

"I know." Ryan pressed his chest against the edge of the table. "You can come help us decorate."

"Hey, buddy, Liz may have other plans. We can't expect her to give us her lights and make her string them too."

Liz spoke before she thought. "Decorating

the tree is my favorite thing to do at Christmas." Shocked at her outburst, she turned to Carter to gauge his reaction. The last thing she wanted to do was push herself on him.

Carter leaned back and looked at her. "How about this? You come join us for the decorating and stay for dinner, then we'll use your lights."

"You don't have to feed me to get the lights."

"Maybe Ryan and I like the idea of having a woman as a guest for a change."

Liz blinked. She'd have thought a man as charming as Carter would have a woman around all the time.

"How about we plan for Sunday at four?" He glanced at Ryan. "That'll give us time to get the perfect tree."

Liz wanted to join them. More than anything. She couldn't turn down the chance even if it had originally been Ryan's idea.

The boy yawned widely. Carter placed his napkin on the table. "I'd better get this guy home to bed."

A few minutes later, they stood outside the restaurant. Carter looked hesitant and touched her arm. "Are you sure you can get home safely? I'll be glad to follow you."

When was the last time someone had worried about her safety? A little over a week ago when Carter had taken her home. He'd done it twice more than any man had in too long. More than capable of taking care of herself, still it was nice to have someone concerned about her. "Thank you, but I'll be fine."

"We'll see you Sunday afternoon?" He looked at her for confirmation.

"I'll be there." She smiled, already looking forward to it.

"Don't forget the lights," Ryan added.

She went down to his level. "I won't. I promise." Once again standing, she looked at Carter.

"I'm glad you joined us tonight. See you Sunday." With a backward wave, he walked away.

"Me too." As she went to her car, she murmured, "Too much."

CHAPTER FIVE

CARTER DIDN'T KNOW what was happening to him. A simple Good Samaritan act in the country club parking lot had turned into meals and time spent with Liz. At first he'd seen them both as two people out of place at a party and now he found he truly liked Liz. His problem had turned into him liking her too much.

The fact Liz had such a good rapport with Ryan made her more appealing. Carter shouldn't have been surprised. From the interactions he'd seen her have, especially with patients, she had a real talent for putting people at ease, understanding and listening to them. Ryan responded to that.

Yet Carter had spent years protecting Ryan from hurt by not bringing women he dated around. He didn't want his son to become attached when he had no intention of making them a permanent fixture in their lives. Somehow Liz had slid under that fence. Even so, he had to keep her at arm's length despite being so enticed by her.

He'd found Liz intriguing to begin with, if a bit standoffish. When he'd invited her to the community meal, it had started out as being friendly, and he'd been looking for an unbiased opinion about the program. After spending a few hours in Liz's company, he'd been impressed with her. His interest had continued to grow the more he was around her. Learning of her sister made his heart go out to her. Something about Liz made him suspect she hid a deep hurt. For some reason that occasional sadness he saw in her eyes touched him. He wanted to make it go away.

Working with her could be exhilarating, as well. As mild-mannered as Liz acted in normal circumstances, she naturally took control in an emergency. As far as he could tell, she could handle any injury with authority and skill.

She'd been more open at the pizza restaurant than he'd ever seen her. Her rapport with Ryan was amazing. Liz seemed to genuinely like his son, be interested in him. Carter liked that about her, as well. It didn't make it easier to keep his distance.

Determined the connection with Liz wouldn't go any further than friendship, he reminded himself that he still didn't know if he could trust her. Could he ever have faith in a woman again? Yet that sexual pull between them had him in its grip. Friendship had become the last thing on his mind. Her dewy pink lips took up more space in his thoughts than they should.

Bringing Liz, or any other woman, into the well-ordered life he'd established with his son wasn't what either of them needed right now. Carter didn't want to tip the fragile scale in the wrong direction. No matter how much he lusted after Liz.

But he couldn't stop himself where Liz was concerned. He might not want to admit it, but he looked forward to every opportunity to see her. Her soft ways and quiet presence eased his fears, made him think of possibilities again. Yes, he didn't want them to become too invested in each other's lives. Liz's background told him she searched for something he couldn't give.

Sunday afternoon Liz pulled into his driveway and he met her in the parking area. She looked unsure until she saw him, and a bright smile came over her face. One that sucker punched him. That reaction he hadn't expected. He'd been looking forward to seeing her much more than he'd realized or found comfortable.

Ryan came running out of the house without a coat or sweater on, or even shoes. Eagerness filled his face, his eyes optimistic. "Did you bring the lights?"

"You need to be dressed for the weather before you come outside," Carter reprimanded.

"I just want to see if she has the lights." Ryan eagerly looked into a window of Liz's car.

"I've got them. They're in the back seat," Liz assured him.

"Great. The tree's up." Ryan hopped around Liz. "Can I see the lights?"

"Go inside," Carter commanded, giving Ryan a nudge. "We'll be right there."

Watching to see if his son did as he ordered, Carter turned back to Liz who had gone to the back-seat door and opened it. She handed him a round plastic top container.

"What's this?" Carter turned the container back and forth, studying it.

"I made another apple pie. I thought the least I could do was bring dessert." She leaned inside the car again and pulled out a sack holding a gallon of ice cream and held it up.

"Okay. I'm officially in love."

A shocked moment hung between them.

A zing of awareness whipped through

Carter that ended in embarrassment. "I'm sorry, that was just a figure of speech."

Liz quickly reassured him. "Oh, I know, I know."

"Hand me the ice cream. You get the lights and let's get in out of the cold." He waited on her and they walked to the house. "By the way, I've your other pie plate all clean and ready to go."

"I'd forgotten about it until I started looking for it to bring this one over." She pushed the back door to the house open and he followed her into the kitchen. "I didn't tell you the other day," she said as she set things down on the kitchen counter, "how much I like your kitchen. Your house is amazing. You've done a beautiful job with it."

"Granny and Pops restored it and updated a couple of rooms before I moved in. Since Ryan and I've been here, we've done more work, but there's only so much you can do with an active boy around. In fact, I have a few small projects outside I've got to get on right away, but I can't depend on Ryan to hold the ladder."

"I could help you with those after we decorate the tree, if you want." Her eyes went wide as if she'd surprised herself by offering.

Carter gave the idea a moment of thought.

"That'd be great. I just need somebody there to call 911 if I fall."

She narrowed her eyes.

"Let's hope it doesn't come to that."

"Dad, come on," Ryan called in an urgent, impatient voice from down the hall.

"On our way, buddy." Carter pushed the pie back from the edge of the counter and grinned. "Wouldn't want that to fall." He turned to the refrigerator, placing the ice cream in the freezer compartment.

Ryan ran in, then jumped up and down. "Can I see the lights? Can I see the lights?"

Liz handed him the box. He dashed out of the room.

"You wait until Liz and I get there before you start putting them on the tree."

She laughed and the sound rippled through him. The pure notes reminded him of bells on a crisp cold day. Heaven forbid he waxed poetic over a laugh. *Wow, this is getting out of hand.* He had to get a handle on himself *now.* "We better get in there before he has the lights in a mess."

Liz headed up the hall and he followed. He could hear Ryan shuffling around and volunteered, "Ryan's been up since seven waiting on you to get here with those lights. I guess I'll have to buy some for next year."

"Just keep these. I'm not going to ever use them. I've a small tree and they're too large for it."

"Thanks. Obviously, they'll be treasured for years to come."

Over the next hour, they worked to get the lights on the tree and put what decorations he had on it.

Carter picked up one of the ornaments. "Look at this one, Ryan. It's the one you made last year in school." His son beamed at him, face aglow in the tree lights as Carter handed it to Ryan to hang.

Carter stood back and studied the tree. "We're a little low on decorations. It looks like we need to do a little shopping."

He hadn't bothered with holiday decorations during his divorce. The custody battle had been his focus. He'd bought a few ornaments over the years afterward, but it wasn't until this year that Ryan had really shown an interest in putting up the tree. What he had to hang on the tree wasn't near enough for its size.

"We can always make some," Liz suggested. "The homemade ones are the best anyway." An odd look came over Liz's face as if she'd said something she shouldn't have.

"Ryan, why don't you put your shoes on and take these empty boxes to the shed?"

"Aw, Dad."

"Go on."

Ryan went to work and soon left.

Carter stepped closer to Liz. "Are you all right? Something happened just a second ago. You want to talk about it? I'm a good listener."

She shrugged. "It's no big deal. I was just remembering something that happened one Christmas."

He waited.

She took a deep breath. "We always trimmed the tree as a family, had a big dinner, then sang carols afterward. I liked it almost better than Christmas Day. Each year Louisa and I'd make a handmade ornament. The same one. When we were about twelve, my mom suggested we should make our own individual one and surprise everyone on decorating night. She was trying to foster our individuality, I think." Liz looked at him with her lips pursed. "See, I was pretty dependent on Louisa. Anyway, we did. I spent a lot of time on mine. Louisa didn't give hers much thought. Mother and Daddy went on and on about how nice mine was. That night before I went to bed, I went to look at it hanging on the tree. It was gone."

"What happened to it?"

"I found Louisa standing over the kitchen garbage can, tearing it up. She didn't see me and I never said anything about it. Until now."

Carter wrapped an arm around her shoulders and gave her a gentle hug.

"I don't know why she did that. She was the one everyone noticed. Except that one time."

Carter knew why. Her sister had been jealous.

Ryan came back into the room and Carter stepped away from Liz.

"Can we make some ornaments like you used to?" Ryan asked, looking from Liz to Carter and back again.

"Ryan, I don't think we need to do that today."

"I'm game, if you are." Liz gave Carter a wry smile.

"You sure?" He didn't want to make this hard on her.

She nodded. "I want to."

Carter gave her a reassuring smile. "Okay. What do we need? I'm about as good at crafts as I am cars."

A grin formed on Liz's lips. To his relief, it reached her eyes. Liz was strong. He'd give her that. She'd already pushed her sadness away.

She looked at Ryan. "That means it's up to us."

Carter put an indigent note in his voice, "Hey, at least I admit my shortcomings."

"And you make up for your shortfalls by being an excellent Good Samaritan."

Carter raised his shoulders and pushed out his chest. "That's more like it."

Liz turned to Ryan. "Do you have construction paper, markers, scissors and glue?"

"I can get the paper and the markers. Daddy has to get the scissors and the glue."

She nodded. "Okay. You go get those and meet me at the kitchen table."

The boy hurried off.

"You're sure you're good with this?"

Her gaze met his. "I'm sure. I didn't mean to bring a good time down a few minutes ago."

"Not a problem. You're a nice person, Liz Poole." In an impulsive move, he placed a soft kiss on her lips. She looked as shocked as he felt. And yet, along with other emotions, he wanted to do it again. Deeper and longer. A little taste wasn't enough. Doing so became overridden by the fear he might have scared her off, but she didn't move.

"Uh, thank you," Liz finally uttered.

He wasn't sure which she'd thanked him for, the compliment or the kiss. It didn't matter.

*   *   *

Liz's body heated as if it were a summer day and the sun beat down from the touch of Carter's lips. She started to speak but stopped when the words wobbled. She cleared her throat and started out of the room. Glancing back, she found Carter watching her.

What had made her think of that awful December day today, of all days? And to tell Carter. He must think her a nut case. For so long she'd chosen not to remember it. Carter had been concerned about her making ornaments again, but she wouldn't disappoint Ryan.

She had just made it to the kitchen when Ryan entered. He put the materials on the table. Liz quickly pushed the salt and pepper shakers and a couple of place mats off to the side. "We're also going to need the scissors."

Carter entered and pulled a drawer out. "Right here."

Ryan scrambled up onto a chair as his dad placed the scissors on the table.

She looked at Carter. "We'll need some glue too."

"I'll get it." He strolled out of the room.

Her attention returned to Ryan who played with the scissors.

"What're we making?" Ryan snapped the scissors closed.

Liz took them out of his hand and set them out of his reach. "We're going to start with something simple like stars."

"How do you make them?"

"I'm going to show you. First, I need to draw a pattern. Then we'll trace around it and cut it out. We can leave it single or add another and make it 3D." Ryan's enthusiasm made her sad memory start to disappear. It would be replaced by a happy one.

"3D?" Ryan wrinkled up his nose.

Liz tapped the end of it with her index finger. "That's when it stands out. Don't worry, I'll show you."

Carter took the chair on the other side of her and placed the glue on the table. His eyes twinkled as he looked between her and his son.

"Hand me a sheet of paper, Ryan." The boy quickly passed one to her. Using a marker, she drew a freehand five-pointed star.

"Wow." Ryan set up on his knees in the chair and looked at her, amazed.

"You are good," Carter agreed.

Liz chuckled. They sure knew how to build her ego. She reached for the scissors. Soon she had the star cut out. "Now, this is our pattern. Hand me another piece of paper." Ryan did so. "Now we trace around this." She placed the star on the paper and asked Ryan, "Will you help me?"

He nodded with comical eagerness, bobbing his head up and down.

"Put your finger right here in the middle." She showed him how she wanted it.

Ryan followed her instructions. She used the marker to draw around the star. "We need to fill up the entire paper, then cut them out. Do you want to trace or cut?"

"I'll draw." Ryan took the marker from her.

"You trace a few, then I can start cutting," Carter offered.

After Ryan had a couple of wavy-lined stars traced, she said, "You're doing a great job."

"You think so?" Ryan looked unsure.

"I know so. Let me cut those that you've done so far, so your father can get started." She cut the paper down the middle. She handed the unused half to Ryan.

Liz pushed the other toward Carter. Their gazes caught. Warmth burned in his eyes. What was he thinking? His hand touched hers as he took it. That electric spark shot up her arm again.

Carter started cutting. "When was the last time you made Christmas ornaments?"

Her gaze met his again. "When I was twelve."

Realization filled his eyes.

"This will be a nice memory to replace the old."

He nodded, compassion in his eyes now. "I'm glad."

"Done," Ryan announced, having filled the rest of the page.

"Then start on another," Liz told Ryan. "It takes twice as many if we make 3D ones."

A few minutes later, they had a small pile of stars.

"We make a pretty good production line," Carter commented.

"What's a production line?" Ryan looked at him.

"It's where one person does one thing, then hands it off to another and so on." Carter returned to his cutting.

"Does Santa use a…a…?"

"Production line," Carter patiently supplied.

"A production line to make toys?" Ryan looked from one of them to the other.

Liz looked at Carter, who had a grin on his face. "Yes, he has a big production line."

Ryan searched his father's face. "The elves help, don't they?"

Carter nodded. "They do."

"Are we Liz's elves?" Ryan's voice had turned thoughtful.

Carter smiled and looked at her. "I believe we are."

Liz laughed and he joined her. She looked around the table. This moment would be the memory she would remember when she thought of making ornaments. The love and warmth between a father and a son, and the feeling of being included in their warmth. They were *her* elves. At this moment she felt special and needed, her world was right.

"We've enough stars. Now I'll show you how to make 3D ones." She picked up two stars. "All you have to do is make a slit halfway on one, then slip it in between two points." She did so. With two fingers, she held it up and twirled it around. "See?"

"Ooh, wow." Ryan looked at her in amazement. "You're smart."

"Thank you, but I can't take the credit. My mom taught my sister and me how to make them."

Carter placed his hand over hers. The prick of pain eased. She gave him a thin smile.

"Look." Ryan held up a 3D star. It was lopsided but he glowed with pleasure.

"That looks wonderful." Liz clapped.

"We can also do circles, if you want to." She took a sheet of paper, drew two circles and quickly cut them out. "You can leave it like this or make it 3D." She split one halfway and inserted another circle. "What do you think?"

"I want to make those too." Ryan reached for a sheet of paper.

"I thought you might." Carter winked at her.

A sweet warmth rippled through her. Liz looked around the table. This was what she had always dreamed of but feared she might not ever find.

She raised a hand. "Not so fast. I've one more to show you." She took a piece of paper and told Carter, "Put your hand out here. Spread your fingers."

He placed his hand on her paper. She gave Ryan the marker. "Now trace around your dad's hand." When he had finished, she pushed the paper to Carter. "Now your part of the production line is to cut it out."

Carter screwed up his face. "It didn't take long to let your job title of Head of Elves go to your head, did it?"

Liz giggled. Something she seemed to do a lot these days.

"Can I do my hand?" Ryan asked eagerly.

Liz picked up the marker. "Sure. I'll trace it."

"Now we need to do yours," Ryan announced, speaking to Liz.

She shook her head. "I don't think you need my hand on your tree."

"Yes, we do. Don't we, Dad?" Ryan gave his father a questioning look.

Carter's look met hers. "Yes, we do."

She blinked, savoring the happiness that washed over her. "Okay, if you want." She placed her hand on the paper and let Ryan trace it.

Carter placed the cut out of Ryan's hand on the table. "What do we do with these after I *painfully* cut them out?"

Liz narrowed her eyes at him. "Yeah, my elves don't complain about their jobs. We'll write our names on them and the year, then they'll be ready to go on the tree." Liz looked at Ryan. "Each year you can add new ones.

"I got one more thing I can show you. How to make a paper chain." Liz placed a star in a pile, picked up a piece of paper and cut off a couple of strips. "Can you pass me the glue, Carter?"

He did so. This time his finger ran along hers as she took the bottle from him. The man was killing her slowly with his touches. "All you have to do is make a loop." She made it. "Place a drop of glue on the ends. Then carefully slip another strip through the center and glue again." She looked at Ryan. "You keep going until you get it as long as you want it. Do you want to try?"

"Yeah."

Liz handed the chain to Ryan. "I'll cut you the strips."

"Remember not to overdo the glue." Carter continued to cut out the traces of their hands.

Ryan sat back in his chair and went to work.

She looked at Carter. He watched her with amazement and something else she couldn't name on his face. *Thank you*, he mouthed.

Unsure where things were heading with them, Liz still feared she was falling for him. While the thought should've scared her, instead it filled her with excitement.

The ringing coming from her phone in her purse ended the moment. She answered it. The voice on the other end of the line she recognized as one from the emergency room. "There's been an auto accident. We need you to consult before the patient goes to the OR."

Liz winced. "I can be there in twenty minutes. Have X-rays, anterior right and left ready for me to review. I'll also need to see all recent blood work." Liz hung up. She hated car accidents. They were the hardest for her to deal with.

"Apparently you're on call." Carter stood beside her.

She gave him a wry smile. "Yeah. You know how it is. When you don't have anything to do, they never call and then you agree to do something... There's been a car accident."

"You got to go?" Ryan asked while he remained busy gluing the chain together.

"I do." Liz went to him. "Why don't you finish up what we started and put them on the tree with your Dad's help? Then I can come back sometime and see how pretty it is."

"You'll come back tonight?"

She looked over his head to Carter, who nodded his agreement. She smiled and nodded to the boy, "I'll try to be back as soon as I can."

"Ryan, we need to let Liz go." Carter picked up her purse and handed it to her. "I'll walk you out."

She opened the door and Carter followed. "I'm sorry. I rarely, if ever, get called. I agreed to help out tonight, thinking it was no big deal. I'll try to get back before Ryan's bedtime. If not, I'll come tomorrow evening. I'm sorry about not holding the ladder for you, as well."

"Don't worry about all that. Just go do what you need to do safely. We'll be here waiting when you get back."

That sounded so perfect. *Waiting on her.*

"I'll save eating the pie until you return."

"You don't have to do that. I might be late. Or I might not get back."

"Then we'll share it for dinner tomorrow." He opened the driver's door for her. When she was in, he closed the door and gave her a little wave.

An hour and a half later, she'd taken care of her patient and was ready to leave the hospital. She waffled about returning to Carter's. Night had fallen, but it wasn't Ryan's bedtime yet. She texted Carter, I'm on my way. Is that okay?

Seconds later her phone dinged. We are waiting.

Liz couldn't help but smile. Soon she turned into the Mooresville community. The backdoor light burned brightly as she pulled to a stop next to Carter's SUV. Ryan ran toward her from the patio where flames flickered in the raised firepit. Carter wasn't far behind Ryan. She wished she came home to this type of welcome every night. She must be careful not to get too involved. Pain lived down that road. But loneliness wasn't much better.

"Liz, you need to come see the tree. It's so pretty." Ryan grabbed her hand. "Come see it from the front, outside. Then we'll go in."

"Hold up a minute, buddy." Carter put his hand on Ryan's shoulder. "Liz, have you had anything to eat?"

"No." She hadn't even thought about food.

"While you and Ryan are around front, I'll warm your plate."

"Can we go now, Dad?" Ryan took her hand again.

Carter nodded. "Yes. Go slow so Liz doesn't fall. It's dark."

She smiled at Carter as Ryan pulled on her hand again. They walked around the house, stopping on the walk facing the front door.

"Isn't it great?" Ryan asked with reverence, as they looked at the tree through the front window. The yellow, red, blue, green and orange lights shone brightly. A blinking star topped it off.

"It is, in fact, the best I've ever seen."

Ryan beamed up at her. She chuckled.

"Now you need to go in and see the decorations. Come on." With the energy only a little boy could have, he went along the walk, then clomped up the front steps and into the house.

Liz hurried after him. She came to stand beside him in the wide doorway of the living room. The tree had indeed been decorated with all the decorations they had made. A paper chain wrapped the tree. There among it all, right up front, was her handprint between Carter's and Ryan's. Her eyes watered. It was the most perfect tree.

"You're right. It's a beautiful tree. The prettiest I've ever seen."

Carter joined them, stepping up beside her, close enough that his heat warmed her. "Are you okay?"

She nodded. "Never been better."

"You sure?" he whispered close to her ear.

"Positive." Her voice becoming stronger.

"Your dinner's hot. I'm going to get Ryan started on his bath and put him to bed while you eat. Sorry I can't keep you company."

"Don't worry about it. I'll be fine. I probably shouldn't have come back. I'll just pack it up and take it home. I'll return your plate."

Carter placed his hands on her shoulders and gave them a gentle squeeze. "Stop, Liz. Ryan and I are glad you're here. Go eat your supper. I won't be long with Ryan." He kissed her temple and left.

Liz stood there a few more minutes, and then with a smile on her face, went to the kitchen.

Carter soon joined her.

"Thanks for this. It was great." Liz indicated the almost-clean plate.

He slid into the chair across from her. "I'm glad you like it."

Ryan entered. "Hey, Dad, can I watch some TV before bed?"

"As long as you don't argue when I tell you it's time to hit the hay. Liz and I are going outside to sit by the fire while we eat our pie."

"Can I—"

"No. You cannot have another piece of pie. Go watch your show and I'll come in and put you to bed in a little while."

Ryan hung his head and left.

Liz laughed.

"Now, about you." His attention didn't leave her. "You want your pie warmed? With or without ice cream?"

"Warm and with ice cream." Liz didn't hesitate to give her order.

"A woman after my own heart. Two pieces of warm pie à la mode."

Liz went to the sink and started washing her dish while he prepared their pie.

"How did things go at the hospital?" Carter pulled the ice cream out of the freezer.

"Not too bad. I just had to make sure a surgery was necessary. The man took a solid hit to the bridge of his nose. I also had to check for any trachea damage. It'll be an uncomfortable holiday season for him, but he won't have any obvious scars."

"Head injuries are never fun. I'm glad the case wasn't too difficult, and you didn't have to stay long. Also I'm glad you got to come back to us." He placed a scoop of ice cream on the pie. "Let's pull on our jackets and have our pie by the fire."

With that done, Carter handed her a plate, picked up his, then opened the door. At the firepit, she took a chair and Carter pulled his up next to hers, but not too close. The clink of his fork against his plate reached her ears as she looked into the fire.

"This is the most amazing apple pie I've tasted. If you decide to give up medicine, you need to go into baking pies."

Carter's comment brought her out of her daze. "I think you're laying it on a little thick, Doctor."

He chuckled as he placed his empty plate on the ground beside the chair. "You're not eating your pie."

She glanced at the plate, then looked at him. "I had too much supper. Would you like to have it? I don't really need it."

"I won't let it go to waste."

She handed her plate over. Liz watched Carter's lips as he pulled a fork between them. He had a great mouth. Full and firm. That one little kiss had made her tingle so much she could only imagine what a real kiss would do to her.

"You really were great with Ryan today. You

saved the day with the decorations. I know it had to have been difficult for you. I really appreciate it."

"It was a lot of fun. Good for me. Cathartic." It had been. She'd enjoyed every minute of it. "Ryan's a great kid. You're doing a wonderful job with him."

"Thanks for saying so. I don't always go to bed thinking that."

She looked at him. "He's seems pretty resilient to me."

"He's had to be with a mom like his." His jaw tightened as an expression of disappointment and anger came over his face.

Liz wasn't sure she should ask but her curiosity got the better of her. "Why?"

Carter looked at the fire instead of her. "Let's just say that she wasn't much of a mother. She was far more interested in herself and her afternoons in bed with her lover."

Liz chest squeezed in pain for what this nice caring man and his child must have endured. "I'm so sorry, Carter. You didn't deserve that."

He continued as if she weren't there. "The worst was I didn't realize she'd been neglecting Ryan until I came home early one day and found him alone in a playpen with a dirty diaper, screaming. I called for Diane and she wasn't anywhere to be found. Here I was with panic filling me that something had happened to her when she comes in the back door, buttoning her shirt with the guy next door behind her. They had obviously been having a quickie."

Liz gripped the chair arm, relieved she hadn't eaten the pie or she might have lost it when her stomach roiled. She placed a hand over his. Carter turned his so their fingers laced.

"I'm glad it's over and done with. She didn't even fight me for custody. She never wanted to be a mother." Disgust surrounded his words.

Feeling indigent on Carter's behalf, Liz sat straighter. "Doesn't sound like she was one anyway. It's her loss. Ryan's a fine boy. Fun to be around. You're a good father and he can feel it."

Carter squeezed her hand. "Thanks for that."

They sat in silence, processing what had been said for a few minutes.

Carter stirred. "I need to put Ryan to bed. Do you want to come in or stay out here?"

"I'll go in. I can say good-night. Then I'd better go." She stood.

"Please wait until I get Ryan to bed before you do." Carter picked up the plates.

"Okay."

Inside Carter put their plates in the sink,

and she followed him into a small den area she hadn't seen before. One large wall had built-in shelves filled with books. There was a cushioned couch and two large stuffed chairs. A desk sat in front of a window. This could only be Carter's private study. Clearly it was here he and Ryan lived the most.

Curled in one of the chairs, Ryan lay sleeping. Carter scooped him up and brought him against his chest. Everything about the action screamed safe and secure.

Feelings she'd always dreamed of finding with a man. She must be careful not to expect more than Carter might be willing to give. Still, a girl could dream of being under Carter's umbrella of care. Finding that perfect place.

CHAPTER SIX

CARTER RETURNED DOWNSTAIRS to find Liz in the kitchen cleaning up the mess from making decorations that he and Ryan had left on the table. Their dessert plates were already in the dish drainer. Efficiency must be her middle name.

"You don't have to do that."

"I don't mind. I helped make the mess." She kept working, not looking at him. "I'll finish up and then go."

He went to the sink and filled a large glass with water. "I need to make sure the fire's out. I'll be right back."

"Okay."

When he returned, Liz was moving the place mats back into place.

"Leave that." He took her hand and led her to the living room where all the lights were off except for the tree. "Let's sit and enjoy the lights for a few minutes. I'd like to know what's going on in that head of yours."

"Nothing."

They settled on the couch but not too close and not touching. He didn't want to scare her off. He huffed. "I can't believe a woman as intelligent as you has nothing on her mind."

"I was just thinking how pretty the tree is. You guys did a great job."

Why he pushed her so, he didn't know. Something about Liz made him think she needed a friend, needed to feel needed, wanted someone to share her thoughts with. Why he believed he should be that person he had no idea, but he couldn't stop himself.

"It wasn't us that made it look great. We just followed your lead. By the way, I saw those tears you were holding back when you saw it. What was that about?"

"I think you need to have your sight checked."

Carter cupped her chin and turned her face toward him. "You aren't a good liar, Liz Poole."

She sighed. "I enjoyed making the ornaments with you and Ryan. It was special. For me, Christmas has already come. Today was a real gift." She nodded toward the tree. "To be included."

"Included?" What could she be talking about? She had been included all day.

"Y'all hung my hand along with yours."

"Sure, we did." Why did she think they wouldn't? "You showed us how to make them. We wouldn't leave you out."

Her gaze met his. "Thank you for that."

"You're welcome." He continued to hold her gaze. "You don't like feeling left out, do you?"

She looked down, picking at a fingernail. "Who does?"

He nodded thoughtfully. "That's true, but something tells me you feel it more acutely than most."

"I got over that a long time ago."

Carter knew that wasn't true. Her behavior at the community party and the expression on her face when she'd arrived at the Mooresville Christmas event said something different. "How's that?"

He feared that she might not answer by the look of apprehension on her face, but she said, "Let's just say I wasn't the party animal growing up. If it hadn't been for my sister seeing that I was invited, I might never have gone to anything."

"That was nice of her." Much more so than the ornament story. "Would you tell me what happened to her?" He really wanted to know, to understand Liz.

He sensed more than saw the tension in her body. Apparently she didn't like talking about her sister, yet she had mentioned her a number of times.

"She was killed in a car accident. She'd been to a party and was on her way home. She took a turn too fast, rolled over." Her words trailed off with all the pain Liz must have lived through at her sister's loss.

Carter took her hand. He didn't have words for what could only have been a horrendous experience. "I'm sorry. That must have been... I can't even imagine. And you had to go to an auto accident today. That can't be easy either."

"It isn't, but it must be done. Louisa's death completely changed my life." She looked at their hands as if studying them for details to complete a painting.

His heart went out to her. He thought a painful marriage breakup had been bad, but to lose a sibling... Somehow, he knew she needed to talk about it. "I bet it did, I can't imagine what I'd do if I lost my brother."

"Louisa was always the shining light in the room. If you had asked her to play the part the other night, she would've jumped at it and asked what she needed to say. I was the geeky one of us." She gave him a weak smile. "I wasn't very good at sports. You know, I was that person who was always the last to be picked. Totally socially awkward. Not Louisa."

Carter gave her hand a gentle squeeze.

Liz took a deep breath and slowly continued, "We were the exact opposite. Everyone loved her. She was the one people were drawn to. With her gone, I lost all of my social life, except for my book club, which she thought was a waste of time and the chess club, which she called *The Dull Club*. Without Louisa, it became clear that I didn't fit in."

Carter inhaled an audible breath but said nothing. He hurt for her. Her sister hadn't given her a chance to shine. The one time she had, Louisa had been jealous.

"Louisa was the one who wanted to be an ears, nose and throat doctor. I always liked the excitement of emergency medicine. She begged me to become an ENT too. That way we could start a practice together." Liz let out a dry chuckle. "Dr. Poole and Dr. Poole, your ears, nose and throat doctors and always glad to see you."

Carter couldn't help but chortle.

Her tone lightened. "We used to giggle over it all the time too."

"So, you became the doctor Louisa wanted

to be, but you do the emergency work through volunteering because that's who you are." Carter winced at the note of disappointment he'd let slip into his voice.

She slumped. "I guess you could put it that way. Louisa always gave me a hard time about using my off time *messing with blood and gore*. Even before she died, I'd thought about leaving the practice and doing emergency work but I couldn't disappoint her." She shrugged. "I'd probably have to do some refresher classes anyway. Now, somehow I feel I'd be disloyal if I closed the practice."

No, she wouldn't. He'd guess Louisa would like knowing she controlled Liz even from the grave. But he couldn't say that. "Life is short they say. I'd hate to know I wasn't doing what I loved."

"I know, but if I give up the practice, that means Louisa is truly gone. I just can't seem to do that."

Carter gathered her into his arms and kissed her on the top of her head. "You don't have to make any decisions tonight."

Liz looked at him. "I'm sorry I dropped all of that on you."

"Not a problem. What're friends for?"

"We're friends?" She pulled away and looked at him. Wonder filled her words.

"Of course we're friends."

"I like the sound of that." She wore a bright smile. "Tell me about your plans for Christmas, friend. Will your family be getting together?"

"You already know my brother is overseas. He'll be home in June on leave and we'll see each other then."

"What about your parents? You going there? They coming here?"

There it was. She'd asked a question he didn't want to answer. A side of him he didn't want to talk about. Was ashamed of. Especially since it was so irrational. How could he not answer after Liz had shared her pain? She deserved an honest answer. "I don't see too much of my parents."

Her brow wrinkled. "Not even at Christmas?"

"No."

"Why?" she asked softly, as if she feared overstepping but her curiosity got the better of her.

Carter let out a deep breath. "I really disappointed my parents when my marriage failed. It's in their eyes whenever I see them. I still can't face them. They've had this perfect long marriage. They expected that of me. And Ryan. Their concern for Ryan hurts. They worry about his mother leaving him. The fact I'm a single parent. It's just easier to not do the—" he used air quotes "—happy family thing. I just can't deal with it."

"I'm sure they don't feel that way."

"Maybe not but it's the way I feel. I can't get past it."

She rested her hand on his thigh for a second. "Our feelings are our feelings. I should know. Will Ryan see his mother?"

"No. She hasn't made an effort in years." He was happy to have it that way.

"How sad. She has no idea what she's missing."

"She's made it clear she has no interest in being a mom or my wife." The bitterness still hung in his words.

"Did you know that before you married her?"

How like Liz to speak her mind. She might not say much but when she did, she came to the point. She didn't seem to have a deceiving bone in her body. That he could appreciate. "She told me she wanted children when what she really wanted was to be a doctor's wife. After Ryan arrived, I started to see differently but by then it was too late. The one good thing she did was give me Ryan."

"I'd never leave my child. Never."

"I can't imagine you would. Your compassion for others goes too deep. Your heart's too big."

"Thank you." She looked at the tree. "You know, this might be the prettiest tree I've ever seen." Liz's words had a soft sigh to them.

It was good not to hear sadness in her voice anymore. "All because of you."

Liz moved to the edge of the couch. "I didn't do much, but I enjoyed it. Every second. I'd better be going."

"I'll walk you out."

Carter stood and offered her a hand. She placed hers in his and he tugged her to her feet. His hands moved to rest on her waist. His gaze met hers before hers flickered away. "Liz?"

He waited until she refocused on him. "I want to kiss you."

She didn't say anything, and his mouth found hers. Her lips were lush and full and everything he dreamed they might be. She stepped closer and pressed against him. He gathered her closer. He took the kiss deeper, his tongue running along the seam of her mouth. She hesitated a moment before she opened for him. A thrill ran through him, making his manhood thicken. She tasted of sweetness and goodness and everything wonderful.

Wrapping his arms around her waist, he lifted her against him. She molded to him as if she'd been made just to fit him. Her hands crawled through his hair as she held his lips to hers.

Liz had fire in her. A fervor he wanted to explore, experience.

Just as quickly as she had kissed him, she backed away. "I can't do this."

"Why not? It seemed to me you were doing it pretty well."

Her look met his. "I don't think we're looking for the same thing."

"Maybe not, but I thought we were friends." She licked her lips.

Carter suppressed a groan. Did Liz have any idea what she did to him? He doubted it.

"Friends don't usually kiss like that. I don't want to be hurt."

"I won't hurt you, Liz."

"You won't mean to, but it'll happen."

He watched her. "That's a very cynical way to look at a simple kiss."

"For me, no kiss is simple."

Before he could respond to that, she'd made it to the kitchen, picked up her purse and pie plate, and was headed out the door.

"Liz…"

"Bye, Carter."

* * *

Liz sat behind her desk on Friday afternoon filling out a form for a patient regarding their working abilities.

She hadn't heard from Carter all week. She wasn't surprised, friends or not. Why would he want to have anything to do with her after the way she had left things? He must think her emotionally stunted.

Rarely had she spoken of Louisa to anyone since she'd died. Not even her mother. It was too hard for both of them. In fact, she'd said Louisa's name more in the weeks since she had met Carter than she had in months. For some reason she wanted him to know about her. Through Carter, Liz had a window to her beloved sister. Louisa had been the other half of her. Part of who she was and would always be.

When she'd mentioned she chose to become an ENT and stayed one because that had been what Louisa had wanted and would want, there had been a note in Carter's voice that made her think he might have been saddened by her decision. Had she been right?

All that didn't matter now. She probably wouldn't ever see Carter again.

Melissa entered Liz's office and flopped down in the only other chair in the tiny room.

"Well, have you heard from the hunky doctor again?"

"No." Liz didn't want to talk about it. She'd broken down and told Melissa about her and Carter's kiss. Melissa had squealed and hugged Liz, telling her how proud she was of her.

"I doubt I will after telling him my life history. Too much sharing, too soon. Once again, socially inept."

"Come on, Liz, don't you think you're being a little too hard on yourself?"

"Maybe. The kiss was good. Really good." Liz even heard the dreamy note in her voice. Carter had reached out and captured her heart like no other. She relived that kiss over and over during the day and in her dreams.

Melissa chuckled. "You should hear yourself. This guy has really gotten to you." She slapped her knee. "I'm glad to see it."

"Yet I've not heard from him since. It doesn't help that I told him I didn't want to be hurt. That's like saying I want to get married. Which I'm pretty sure, after his last marriage, he isn't planning to do for a long time. I'm sure he has run for the hills."

She'd had a special time making decorations with Carter and Ryan. For once she'd felt included, valued. Maybe she needed to chalk it up to a good time had while it lasted. The problem was she wanted more of them. For Carter to kiss her again. And again.

Melissa met Liz's look and grinned. "The weekend isn't here yet. Got to go. See you Monday. Hang in there and don't do anything I wouldn't do if he calls. And he will call."

Liz had already come to the conclusion she'd be back to spending quiet weekends at her condo. What bothered her the most was how she'd so easily become involved in Carter and Ryan's lives. Hers seemed gray in comparison. Returning to her solitary life wouldn't be easy this time.

An hour later when her phone rang and Carter's name showed up on the ID, her heart did a tap dance against her rib cage. Her hand shook as she picked up the phone.

"Hello." She forced her voice not to quiver.

"Hey there. How're you doing?" Carter sounded as if days hadn't passed between them or that kiss.

Liz wished she could be so cool. "I'm fine. You?"

"Great. I'm sorry I haven't had a chance to give you a call this week. Ryan and I had a couple of things going on at his school."

Carter didn't have to make excuses, but she appreciated them. At least it hadn't been her oversharing that had kept him away.

"I was wondering if I offered you dinner tomorrow, would you consider holding the ladder for me? That's if you're not busy." Finally he sounded a little unsure. "I was gonna get someone around here to do it, but John still has the burned arm and the Wilsons have gone to their daughter's for the weekend since it's so close to Christmas. They're predicting rain and maybe snow, and I need to get this done."

He didn't have to sell her. She didn't care what excuses he had. She wanted to help. To see him again.

"What're friends for?"

"I promise to keep it that way." He sounded sincere.

A prick of disappointment stuck her. "I can be there tomorrow afternoon around three. Will that work?"

"Yeah, that'll work. I'll come up with something for us for dinner." He sounded uncertain as if he wasn't sure what that might be.

"Why don't you let me bring it? I'll pick up some fried chicken." Liz ran through a list of places she could stop on her way.

They settled on one.

"That sounds great." Happiness filled Carter's voice.

Maybe he hadn't been so sure about her.

With her heart doing an extra tip-tap, she said, "I'll see you tomorrow afternoon then."

"All right. Hey, Liz..." Carter's voice dropped low.

"Yes?"

"I'm looking forward to seeing you again." Her heart fluttered. She ended the call with a smile and a sigh of happiness. He still wanted to see her, even if it was just to get her help. Still, she would take that. At least he thought there was more to her than the crazy person she'd been the other day. She valued his friendship and wanted to keep it.

The next afternoon, Liz arrived at Carter's as scheduled with a bucket of fried chicken and all the sides that went with it. Her body tingled with the anticipation of seeing him.

"I see you're dressed to go to work." Carter came down the back steps to greet her in the parking area.

She had pulled her hair back, wore a long sleeve shirt with a navy quilt zip-up vest and jeans along with sports shoes. "Didn't you say you were going to put me to work?"

He stepped to the car. "I did. I appreciate you being willing to help me out."

"Not a problem." She reached in the car and pulled the food out.

Carter took it from her as Ryan came bounding down the steps. "Hey, Liz."

Her smile broadened. He'd dropped the "Miss" to the more familiar first name. She liked that. "Hey there, Ryan."

The boy ran to her for a hug. She gave it. He then looked at Carter. "Daddy, I'm going to play in the square with the guys, okay?"

Liz watched as Carter's smile dropped and a shadow of reluctance formed in his eyes. He looked out at the square and then back at his son, disquiet obvious in his features. "Okay but stay where I can see you. Liz brought us dinner and it'll be time to eat soon."

"Yes, sir." Ryan ran off without a backward glance.

Carter watched him until he joined the boys. Liz followed his look. "That's hard for you, isn't it?"

"Yeah."

"You have given him a good safe place to run and play. So many kids stay inside and are on technology all the time."

His gaze finally returned to her. "It's one of the reasons I wanted to live here."

She studied him a moment. "It's hard to trust your judgment when you've been burnt."

"Yep." Carter made it sound easier than she knew it was for him. He took the bag from her.

"Come in for a sec while I put this away, then we'll get to work."

Liz trailed him into the house. As he set the bulky large bag on the counter, she placed her purse in the seat of a chair.

Done with seeing about the food, he stepped toward her, his look penetrating. For a second she wondered if he might kiss her. Instead he blinked and the look disappeared.

"I think we'd better get to work before I change my mind about doing so." Carter opened the door.

Liz shook her head. She needed a moment to recover, refocus. She swallowed. "I'm ready."

His eyes twinkled as she passed him. "By the way, you look cute."

Cute? She couldn't remember anyone ever telling her she looked cute. Coming from Carter, she liked the compliment.

"I wasn't sure how to dress but I figured comfort should be the way to go."

"It is. I already have the ladder against the house. I just need you to steady it while I climb up. Before I get started, I'll just check on Ryan." He walked to the corner of the house and soon returned.

Carter pulled from a tool bag a hammer and a small bag of nails. He started up the ladder.

"Are you sure I'm the right person for this

job?" Liz wasn't confident she'd be much help based on her size versus his. "Even though I used to help my father with stuff like this."

"I could've probably handled it on my own, but this type of work you shouldn't do alone. A doctor who does as much emergency work as you should know that."

"You're right about that. I see too many accidents from thoughtless mistakes." She put her foot on the bottom rung of the ladder and placed her hands firmly on the side rails as Carter climbed higher. She watched Carter's progress with an excellent view of his backside encased in worn jeans she could only describe as amazing. Yes, she had been given a good job.

"Hopefully this won't take very long. I'll have to move the ladder a couple more times, then that'll be it." He pulled the nails out of his pocket.

She watched him. "You be careful with that hammer. Don't drop it on my head."

"I promise not to. That would be an example of a thoughtless mistake."

"That it would, so don't do it," she told him in no uncertain terms.

Carter secured the board that had come loose with a couple of nails and started down the ladder. "This wouldn't be such a big deal, but I'm afraid it's going to start raining soon and the next thing I know I'll have a problem with rot. You know how it is this time of the year in north Alabama, a lot of rain, freezing cold days and now the weatherman's predicting snow. I didn't want to wait any longer."

By the time Carter reached her, she'd again been treated to an up close and personal view of his behind. As he got to her, the ladder slipped a bit. She applied more pressure to the bottom rung, steadying it. Carter had to step through her arms.

His bottom brushed along her chest. Carter was all firm and delicious male. Her breathing picked up as blood whizzed through her veins. Not soon enough and too soon, he stood on the ground. She wasn't thinking friendly thoughts. Quickly she moved away.

Carter looked at her and grinned. "I'd no idea I'd enjoy this repair work so much."

Liz giggled like a silly girl. "Are you taking advantage of the situation?"

His gaze bored into hers. "If I were, I'd be kissing you right now out here in front of God and everyone but I keep my promises. We'll remain just friends until you decide differently."

Liz gulped. "Oh."

Carter handed her the hammer, then scooted

the ladder along the side of the house a few feet. He found a level piece of ground and stopped. "I've this one and one more to do. Then there're a couple of little spots on the porch, but they don't require this long ladder."

Liz looked above the ladder to see a large board sticking out that obviously needed securing. Taking the hammer from her, Carter once again climbed and proceeded to take care of the problem. He added more nails than before. Every time he swung, the ladder shook.

Tightening her grip, Liz applied additional body weight to keep it steady.

Carter returned to the ground safely only to do it all over again. He made another trip down. "That's the worst done. Now let's take care of the porch." Carter picked up his tool bag and started toward the front of the house. "Would you mind being the muscle while I hammer?"

"Sure." Liz fell into step with him. "I'm afraid I might not be much muscle."

Carter squeezed her upper arm. "I think you'll do."

He made that sound like he might be talking about more than just being handyman help.

On the porch, Carter let the bag drop to the floor. "If you'll just push right here." He placed his hand near the end of a board with a corner sticking out. "Just beside mine."

She did as he asked. It brought her body along beside his from shoulder to foot. Awareness shot like electricity through her. Carter acted as if the position was the most natural in the world as he put three nails in the board.

"There. That's great." He straightened.

Liz missed the firmness of him pressed against her.

"I'll need help with this next one, as well." They moved to another spot on the other side of the door. They assumed the same position.

Again, Liz's body hummed at his touch. She let Carter get to her, and she shouldn't do that. Too soon, he finished. Disappointment washed over her.

"There's one more spot over here." Carter moved a chair out of the way. He placed his hand on the wall.

She assumed the position again. Looking over his arm, she studied the spot he should be working on. "I thought you said there were only a couple of spots. This doesn't look bad."

"You're right, there's nothing wrong with it. I just liked having your body up against mine."

Liz giggled and stepped away, giving him a light swat on the arm. "Here I was trying to help you and you're busy taking advantage of me. Friends don't treat each other that way."

Carter's eyes bored into hers. "If I plan to take advantage of you, I'll make it clear that's what I'm doing. Being around you makes it hard to just be friends."

Her mouth went dry. Molten heat ran through her.

He stood quickly and repositioned the chair before picking up his tool bag. "I need to put this up in the shed and hang the ladder up, then we'll have supper." He grinned at her as if nothing had just happened. "Hey, I really appreciate your help."

"You're welcome. I'm not really sure I was needed." Still it was nice to have him think she had been necessary.

"You're good help. Do you mind carrying my tool bag while I get the ladder?"

She picked up his bag and staggered for a second until she adjusted to the weight. "Do you have every tool known to man in here?"

He shrugged. "It never hurts to be prepared. I like working on the house. It's a nice difference from practicing medicine."

"Apparently you're pretty good at it. It looks well cared for."

He seemed pleased with her statement. "I try, but it's an ongoing project. Today's an example." Carter glanced over his shoulder toward the square.

Liz looked as well, finding Ryan along with two more boys playing chase. "Does Ryan ever ask about his mother?"

"Not really. Not anymore." Carter's tone implied relief.

"I have a good mother, though she's not always great to deal with, but I wouldn't want her not to be around."

"He's better off without her." Bitterness hung in Carter's words. In that area he'd not moved on.

Maybe she should leave it alone, but she couldn't seem to. "What if he starts asking questions again?"

"I'll deal with that when it comes. Right now, he's my life's focus."

As in Carter didn't have room for anyone else in his life? "Ryan's a great kid. You've done a wonderful job with him."

"Thanks. Right now, I need to call him in to eat." Carter whistled, loud.

Ryan stopped and looked in their direction, then said something to the boys before heading their way.

Liz looked at Carter in wonder. "That's a neat trick."

"Yeah. I practiced an entire summer before

I got it. It does come in handy. I usually stand out on the front porch and whistle. Ryan comes running."

"My dad whistled but not that loudly."

"You've not told me anything about your father really. Where's he?"

"He died almost five years ago from cancer. Between losing him and Louisa, it's been a tough few years. I miss him every day. He was my number one cheerleader." To her amazement, she continued, "Louisa might have been the apple of Mom's eye, but Dad made me feel special. I didn't, still don't, always measure up to my mom's expectations. Mom has a hard time accepting that."

Carter mouth pursed as he gave her a searching look. "Even after you became a doctor?"

"Yeah." Liz huffed. "Now her problem is that I'm not married with a family."

Carter faced her. "I think you're pretty amazing."

"You don't have to try to make me feel good. I accepted how things were a long time ago." She didn't want his pity or him saying nice things just because he thought he should.

"I can assure you, I mean it."

"You've given me more compliments in the last few days than I've had in years."

He started walking again. "More people should be complimenting you."

Liz smiled. With the firmness in Carter's tone, she might start to believe it.

CHAPTER SEVEN

CARTER STEPPED BEHIND the shed located adjacent to the parking area and hung the ladder on its hooks. Liz stood off to the side, watching him.

He glanced at her. A look of wonder covered her face. She held her palm up. "It's snowing."

Liz looked beautiful, angelic. A fat flake landed on her face and she brushed it away.

For a moment earlier, he had felt sorry for Liz, but he knew she didn't want that. It made him angry on her behalf that her mother couldn't see the amazing person she was. That her sister had taken advantage of her good nature. Now Liz looked so happy. He had to control his urge to pick her up and swing her around.

Instead he took the tool bag from her, opened the shed door and went inside. Liz waited outside. Placing the bag on the workbench, he headed out again. Liz backed away to give him room to exit. When she did, one of the pavers in front of the door tipped and she fell. Her hands flew up, but Carter wasn't able to catch her. Instead her body twisted and she went down on her backside.

"Liz!"

He went to one knee beside her. "Have you broken anything? Let me check."

"I'm fine."

Embarrassed, her eyes wouldn't meet his. "Don't move. Let me check for any broken bones."

She glared at him, all stubborn woman. He couldn't help but admire that. Liz stretched her hand out toward him. "I'll take a hand up."

Carter stood, then pulled her to her feet.

"Ow." Liz gripped his forearm as she held her right foot off the ground.

"You did hurt yourself." Carter didn't bother asking before scooping her into his arms.

"What're you doing?" she sputtered with indignation.

"I'm carrying you into the house," Carter said flatly.

Liz pushed against his shoulder. "I can walk."

He tightened his grip. "Yeah. I just saw you in action."

Ryan came running up. "What happened?"

"She fell. Go hold the door." The boy raced off. To Liz, Carter said, "You can stop struggling. I'm not putting you down until we get inside." He adjusted her against his chest. "It'll only make carrying you more difficult if you struggle."

Liz settled, putting an arm around his neck, making it easier to hold her. The slight floral aroma of what he guessed must be her soap found his nose. Underlying that, and much more tantalizing was the scent of Liz. He inhaled. That smell he'd forever associate with her.

She felt good against him—warm, all woman, right. Maybe too much so.

"I could've walked." That nervous sound in Liz's voice had returned.

"Maybe so, but I like this better." He took the first step to the back door. Why did he keep saying things like that to her? Because he meant it. He'd started to care beyond friendship.

She looked down. "Don't you drop me going up these stairs."

Carter took another step. "Oh, ye of little faith."

"I'll remind you of that when we're both at the bottom of the steps in a tangle."

"Mmm, that sounds nice. If you don't hush,

I might trip on purpose." His lips brushed her ear. The shiver going through her pleased him. "Hold the door wide, Ryan."

Ryan did as he was told. Carter turned to the side so he and Liz could enter without too much of an issue. He set her on her uninjured foot while she held the other up. Jerking a chair over, he helped her to sit. Carter pulled another close before gently lifting her painful foot up to rest on the chair.

"Don't move until I've made sure you haven't broken anything."

"I can check." She leaned forward.

He placed a hand on her shoulder and nudged her back. "This time you're the patient. I'm the doctor."

Liz released a long-suffering sigh as he went to one knee and started to remove her shoe.

Ryan came up beside him. "What's wrong?"

"Hey, buddy, would you look under the sink in the hall bathroom and bring me the first aid kit. You know, the one we put up the other day after Mr. John got hurt."

"Yes, sir." He left like a rocket.

Carter carefully slipped off Liz's shoe and let it drop to the floor. He did the same with her sock. A blue spot had already formed on the left side of her ankle.

Ryan returned with the first aid kit as Carter examined Liz's foot by slowly running his fingers over her ankle area, applying pressure here and there. She winced only when he came near the discolored area.

"I believe you've a sprain here." Carter stood.

Liz sighed. "That's what I thought."

He reached for the box and pulled it to him. "I'm going to put on an elastic bandage. Then we'll ice it and keep it elevated."

"I'll go home and do that." She moved to raise.

Carter gave her a pointed look. "What's it they say about doctors making the worst patients?" He shook his head. "Don't be one of those. You can't drive and if you haven't noticed, it has started to snow heavily."

Liz swiveled in the chair toward the window. "So quickly?"

Carter shrugged. He opened the box and pulled out a thick roll.

Ryan stood nearby, watching wide-eyed as Carter wrapped Liz's ankle. "Now for an ice pack." Carter went to the freezer section of the refrigerator and pulled out another bag of peas, returned and placed them on her ankle.

"Ooh, I don't like those." Ryan wrinkled up his nose.

Carter and Liz laughed.

"That's what I've heard," Liz said.

He ruffled his son's hair. "It's a good thing you don't because otherwise we wouldn't have any ice packs. They'll go to better use on Liz's foot than in your belly."

She smiled. "Glad I could help you out."

"Now you sit there while I get our supper on the table." Carter turned to the counter. "Ryan, you go wash your hands, then come back and set the table."

Ryan headed out of the kitchen without complaint.

"I hate it, but I need to do the same." Liz held up her hands.

"You sit right there. I'll get you a wet rag."

Carter turned to the sink, pulled a dishrag out of a drawer and wet it, then handed it to Liz.

Liz began cleaning her hands. "I'll give these peas about thirty minutes, then I'll head home before it gets worse outside."

Carter pointed with a thumb out the glass. "I think your window of opportunity has been lost. Even with this much snow, the road will be messy and the bridge icy. Especially the one between here and the highway. You're stuck with us for the night at least."

Liz reared in the chair. "I can't stay here!"

"Why not? I assure you that Ryan and I are gentlemen."

She moaned. "I know that but..."

"Complain all you want but I don't think it's a good idea to drive right now. I promise to make you comfortable. Now let's get this food on the table." Carter pulled the cartons out he'd placed in the refrigerator earlier. After opening them, he put them in the microwave to heat. He undid the bucket of chicken, then looked at Liz. "Do you like your chicken warm or at room temperature?"

"I'm happy with it right out of the box."

Ryan ran into the room and slid to a stop. "Dad, it's really snowing now."

"Yeah, buddy, it is. How about getting the table set?"

Ryan went to a drawer, grabbing a handful of forks.

"Bring those here and I'll help you." Liz reach out a hand to take the forks from Ryan. "I need to be useful."

Ryan gave them to her and scurried back to get napkins.

When the microwave beeped, Carter carefully took the hot items out and carried them to the table. "Sorry about the unfancy serving dishes."

"No problem. It makes cleaning up easier," Liz assured him.

"Dad, I need plates." Ryan waited near a cabinet.

"I'm on it." Carter pulled three plates from the shelf. He handed them to Ryan and watched as he slowly and carefully, with an air of importance, walked to the table.

Liz helped him place them. She fit in well in his house. Even when she was injured. Too well.

"Ryan, if you'll take this bucket of chicken over to the table, I'll get the drinks and we should be all set." Carter quickly filled two glasses with iced sweet tea and a smaller one with milk. He placed them on the table, taking a chair next to Liz. Ryan took the one at the end of the table since Liz had her foot on the other chair.

"Please let me serve since I've been little to no help with getting this meal on the table." Liz picked up a plate.

"Hey, you've a good reason." Carter handed her a serving spoon. His fingertips brushed over the back of her hand as she took it. At her soft hiss, he smiled.

* * *

Liz had enjoyed watching, helping where she could, as Carter and Ryan worked to get their dinner on the table. There was something pleasant about being in a warm kitchen with it snowing outside and seeing two males work together to get a meal together. Her home seemed sad and lonely compared to this one. Being around Carter and Ryan made her wish for a family more. It was everything she wanted in life. The type of thoughts she shouldn't have regarding Carter.

Her staying the night wasn't a good idea, but she couldn't in good conscience ask Carter to bundle Ryan up and drive around on slick roads for her. She couldn't drive with a messed up right foot. As anxious as she was about the arrangements, she couldn't come up with another plan.

As they ate, Ryan went on and on about getting to play in the snow the next day. "Dad, can we build a snowman?"

"Sure, we can," Carter answered between bites of food.

"Liz, have you ever built a snowman?" Ryan looked at her.

She wiped her mouth with a napkin. "I have, but a long time ago."

Carter's cell phone rang. He went to answer

it and put it on speaker. "Hey, Carter, this is Joey's mother. Joey wants to know if Ryan would like to come spend the night with him and play in the snow in the morning?"

Ryan twisted in his chair. "Can I, Dad?"

Carter glanced at her. Liz wasn't sure if he was asking for her okay or not.

Ryan got to his feet and jumped around Carter. "Come on, Dad. I promise to use my manners."

Placing a hand on the boy's shoulder, Carter made him stand still. "Okay, I'll let you go but you must be on your best behavior." Carter said into the phone, "He'd like to come but he needs to help me clean up supper, bathe and pack. I'll have him there in about an hour. Will that work?" A few seconds later, Carter ended the phone conversation.

"May I be excused?" Ryan asked.

"Yes," Carter told him. "Go get a bath. I'll get your sleeping bag, then be up to help you get your warm clothes together."

Ryan dumped his plate in the sink with a rattle and hurried out of the room. Carter's concerned look landed on her. "I hope you don't think I planned this."

"That never occurred to me." She meant it. He'd made her a promise and she trusted him to keep it.

* * *

Carter wasn't surprised. Liz believed in the goodness of people. She wouldn't think he'd take advantage of her. She believed in him. He wouldn't let that go unhonored even if it killed him. "We need to take this ice off for a while. I'll get you settled by the TV and then go help Ryan"

"I'll see about myself. Don't worry about me. You take care of Ryan. I'm fine right here."

"Don't you get up and start cleaning the kitchen. You need to stay off that foot. How about I put you in there in front of the TV and you check the weather?"

"I'm fine, Carter. Go on." She waved him away. "It's just a little sprain."

"Yeah. One done while helping me."

Liz shifted in the chair. "I wasn't helping you at the time. It's my own stupidity for not watching what I was doing."

He smiled half-heartedly. "I don't think either one of us is gonna win this argument."

"Dad," Ryan called from above.

"I'm gonna go help Ryan. Retreat is the better part of valor."

Liz nodded. "Go. I'll be here when you get back."

Carter pointed a finger at her. "You'd better stay put."

"I think you're taking giving orders too seriously, Doctor."

Carter glared at her. Liz would do as she wished no matter the orders he gave. Stubborn woman.

She returned a serene smile.

Carter took the stairs two at a time. It was best just to see to Ryan and hope Liz didn't do any further damage to her ankle. Fifteen minutes later he returned to the kitchen with Ryan's bag over his shoulder and Ryan trailing behind him. To his great amazement, Liz still sat where he'd left her but his and her plates had been stacked and the food containers were consolidated, ready for the garbage.

"I see you've been busy."

She gave him the same serene smile as earlier. "Yep, but I still followed the doctor's orders."

Carter narrowed his eyes. "If I were to guess, you were tempted not to."

She raised both shoulders and let them fall.

"Let's go, Dad. Let's go." Ryan stood in the hallway.

"Give me a sec to get Liz settled in front of the TV. Then we'll head out. Why don't you turn on the TV and put the remote near my chair?" he asked Ryan, as he stepped toward Liz and scooped her into his arms.

"I could walk." She sounded resigned instead of argumentative.

Her breath flowed over the skin of his neck, making his blood heat. "Maybe so, but I enjoyed last time so much I thought I'd do it again."

She clasped her arms around his neck. That brought her more securely against him. This might not have been such a good idea. Everywhere she touched him burned. His manhood needed a trip out into the cold weather sooner rather than later. He whispered, "You know, I could get used to this."

To his great pleasure, Liz turned a lovely shade of pink. She wasn't as unaffected as she wanted him to believe. She fought the attraction, as well. "You shouldn't."

"You can be hard on a man, Liz."

She looked into his eyes but said nothing.

When they reached the den, he settled her in his chair. Pulling the matching footstool close, he lifted her foot to it, adjusted the peas over her ankle, then handed her the TV remote. "I shouldn't be gone long. Don't get up and move around. I don't want you to fall and make matters worse."

"Let's go. Let's go," Ryan called from the doorway.

On impulse Carter kissed the top of Liz's head. "I'm coming, Ryan."

Liz watched Carter and Ryan leave. The tingle from Carter's unassuming kiss still lingered. She heard the click of the front door closing. The house turned quiet, yet she didn't feel alone. Something about being in Carter's space, the place where he relaxed, made her feel at home.

She settled deeper into the cushions. Her ankle shifted to the side, sending pain up her leg. A sharp reminder she sat here only because of an injury. She needed to keep that in mind. This was unchartered territory for her. She must be careful not to make more of it than it was.

Flipping channels, Liz found the weather channel. It apparently wasn't going to get any better during the night. Carter had been right. She shouldn't be driving. For the time being, she had to stay. The prediction said there'd be a warm up by midmorning. The roads should start clearing enough for her to get home then.

She'd just make the best of it and not be in the way any more than necessary. She imagined there were all types of women who wished they could take her place and here she was worried about spending the night at Carter's. She looked around. It really was a dream come true. Snowbound with a handsome man in a cozy home at night...

She jerked straight at the sound of the door opening.

"Carter?"

"Yeah, it's just me." The sound of his voice flowing down the hallway wrapped around her heart. Would it be so wrong to relax and pretend for one night? Live out a dream.

The double thump on the floor must have been him removing his boots. A swoosh of fabric told her he'd taken off his coat. Seconds later he entered the room, looking gorgeous with his tousled hair and red cheeks. Desire whipped through her. Yes, every woman's dream, especially hers.

"Hey." He sounded out of breath as if he'd hurried back.

"Hey yourself."

He dropped to the sofa, sitting at a right angle to her. "I hope you don't think I planned all of this."

"What? For it to snow?"

"Funny lady. But I don't control the weather. No, about Ryan not being here. I didn't set that up. I just couldn't say no because I've been working so hard for him to feel a part of this place. Joey's family, I trust. He couldn't just go to anyone's house."

Liz clasped her hands in her lap to keep from pushing the lock of hair off his forehead. "I understand. None of this you planned. Particularly me. I think we can handle this. I'm just sorry you have to nursemaid me."

"I don't mind. I hate that you got hurt." He leaned forward and put his elbows on his knees.

She tightened her grip on the arm of the chair. "I don't think it's going to be that bad. I'll probably be fine by tomorrow."

"We'll see. For now, how about a cup of coffee?" He stood.

She looked at him. "Any chance of a hot tea?"

Carter nodded. "I think I can find some. You stay put."

He strolled out of the room. Once more Liz listened to the sounds of his movements in the kitchen and those of the old house. It could be so quiet where she lived. Sometimes it echoed around her. Having someone else around felt nice. The fact it was Carter made it even nicer.

Soon he returned with a mug in each hand. He set the steaming cups on the table beside her. "Would you like some sugar or anything else?"

"No, just tea is fine. Thank you." She picked up the mug and took a careful sip.

Carter retook his place on the sofa. "How's your foot feeling?"

"The throbbing isn't as bad as it was earlier."

He brought his mug to his lips. "That's good to hear. Would you like to watch a TV show, play cards, chess or listen to some music?"

"You don't have to entertain me if you need to be doing something else."

Carter grinned. "I assure you, I've nothing better to do than spend time with you."

"If that's the case, then I do enjoy a good game of chess."

"Chess it is." He stood and went to a shelf. "I'll have to warn you, I'm pretty good at this."

"Then I'll ask you to take it easy on me."

Carter returned with a chessboard. He set it on the stool beside her foot as he moved the table farther out so that it was positioned within arms' reach of both of them. Placing the board on the table, he took a seat on the sofa again. "I promise I will."

"Thank you." She gave him a sly grin. Maybe it wasn't fair for her not to remind him she was a member of a chess club but his self-assured attitude he'd automatically win made her want to surprise him with her abilities. An hour later, she announced, "Check."

After studying the board for a good five minutes, Carter leaned back with a deep sigh. He glared at her. "I've been had. I'm the one who should've been asking you to be kind to me."

She giggled. "I did tell you I'm a member of the local chess club."

He groaned.

"I could've let you win but I thought you'd like that less than if we played an honest game."

"I've learned one more thing about you Liz—you can be sneaky." He grinned.

She returned it. Carter wasn't angry. She was glad. Other men might have been. "I can say you were a worthy opponent."

"Thank you for allowing me a little of my ego. You're good."

"I'm glad you're not mad."

Leaning close, he looked her in the eyes. "You do know that my ego isn't so fragile that I can't take losing to a woman."

Her smile grew and she said in her best southern belle voice, "Why, Carter, that never crossed my mind."

He glared at her. "You, Dr. Poole, are teasing me."

"And you, Dr. Jacobs, are right!"

"Another game?"

Liz yawned and shook her head. "Another time."

"You're tired. We need to put some ice on that ankle again before you go to sleep. How about we get you upstairs and I'll get your bed ready along with finding you something to sleep in?"

"The couch here'll be fine."

Carter stood and picked up the board, returning it to the shelf. "No, it isn't. I want you to be comfortable."

This part of the evening Liz had been questioning. She had no experience in how to act in these types of situations. "I'll be comfortable enough on the couch."

"*This* we won't argue about further." Carter's tone made the statement sound final. "For safety reasons I won't be carrying you up the stairs, but I'll help you. Are you ready to get started?"

She didn't seem to have a choice.

Carter moved the table back into place, then offered her his hand. She took it. He helped her to stand. She put as little pressure on her hurt foot as possible.

"Put your arm around me." His arm went around her waist, bringing her close to his side. "I'll support most of your weight. Okay, you ready to give this a try?"

Liz did as he said. Her fingers grasped the firm muscle beneath them. She liked the feel of him.

"Now hop along and I'll support you."

They made it out of the room and into the hall without a mishap except for her heart beating faster from being so close to Carter.

He flipped on the hall light switch. "The stairs will be a little trickier. I'll take most of your weight as we go up. This is the one time I hate that this old house doesn't have any bedrooms downstairs."

Liz leaned heavily on Carter as they slowly made their way up. Having his support assured her she wouldn't fall. At the landing she was both glad and sad they had made it. Happy because they hadn't had an accident and disappointed because Carter eased his hold.

"Down this way, second door on the right."

Liz knew the moment she saw the bedroom that it belonged to Carter. She jerked to a shocked stop. "This is your room."

"Yes, it is. It's the only one with a bath off it. I'm going to sleep in Ryan's room."

Staying in Carter's bedroom wasn't a good idea. The space was too personal. It made her nervous. Needy. Gave her ideas she shouldn't have. Carter was being considerate to give up his own well-being, but she'd gladly share.

"Come on in. I'll let you have some privacy in the bathroom. But first let me get clean sheets out of the cabinet in there." He led her to the bed. "Sit here while I get them."

He turned on a lamp beside the bed, then walked away.

Liz swallowed hard as she lowered to Carter's bed. "I'm… I'm sorry you're having to go to so much trouble for me."

"Not a problem." His voice carried from the bathroom.

She looked around. The space looked as orderly as the rest of Carter's home. The bed had a large sleigh headboard with big fluffy pillows positioned against it and what looked like a hand-quilted cover on it. She ran her hand over it. A window with a desk and chair sitting in front of it faced the backyard and a large tree beyond the shed. She grinned. The only evidence of disorder were books cluttering the desk. Beside it sat a cushioned chair that appeared far more comfortable than the other one. On another wall was the door to the bath, and beside it stood a tall chest of drawers. An oriental rug covered a great deal of the gleaming wide board floor. All in all, the decor suited the age of the house, and Carter. Every inch she loved.

Carter returned with a bundle of material in his arms and dropped it on the bed.

"Okay, your turn." He put his arm around her.

She limped to the bath.

"I'll find you something to wear. I left some supplies on the sink you're welcome to." Carter left her holding on to the door frame.

She entered the bath, holding on to whatever she could reach, being careful not to slip on the small black-and-white tile floor. Closing the door behind her, Liz looked at the space. It had been modernized but still maintained the flavor of the house with twin pedestal sinks, a large footed bathtub with a curtain to pull around for a shower and a pull-chain commode. It looked historical while being functional. Liz loved it. In fact, the idea of getting to soak in that tub sounded like heaven. With Carter would be nicer...

The knock at the door startled her. She jerked around.

"Hey, Liz, here's something you can sleep in." The door opened and Carter's long arm came through the crack. On the end of one of his fingers hung a navy T-shirt.

Liz took it, grateful he couldn't see the guilt on her face from her wandering thoughts. "Uh, thanks."

"Is something wrong?"

"No, uh, no, I'm fine." Heaven help her, she had to get control of herself. "I was just admiring your tub."

"Call me if you need help. Don't take any chances on falling."

Liz looked at the T-shirt. It'd be plenty big, but she wasn't sure about the length. She shrugged. It was that or sleep in jeans, which wasn't appealing. After taking care of her needs and washing her face, she removed all her clothes except her panties and neatly folded her clothing, placing the pile on a chest between the sinks. She pulled Carter's shirt over her head, taking in his scent. She shivered, then firmly adjusted the shirt to cover her.

Shuffling to the door, she pushed at her hair. She huffed. As if she knew about planning a seduction. The only reason she would be staying in Carter's bedroom was because she had hurt herself. He was just being nice. She'd been the one to establish the friendship rule. But she didn't want friendship tonight. She desired more. Squaring her shoulders she murmured, "Here goes nothing."

Carter straightened from where he'd been picking up a pillow off the floor. He looked at her. His eyes burned brightly before he blinked, and the flames were banked. He flipped the pillow to the bed and came toward her.

Liz had no idea what her reaction would be when he touched her. She might not have a lot of experience, but she could recognize when a man wanted her. Carter did. Excitement developed into a scorching need.

"I have to say without a doubt that T-shirt has never looked that good on me." He offered her his hand. "Let me help you to bed."

She chuckled.

Carter glanced at her. "What's up?"

"You've a way of using come-on lines without knowing it. You did it all the time when we first met."

"Huh?"

"Stuff like, *let me help you to bed*. It sounded like a come-on."

His forehead wrinkled. "I didn't mean for it to be a come-on." Carter paused. When his look returned to hers, his eyes had heated as before. "Unless you wanted it to be?"

She glanced at the bed and back to him.

Carter swung her up into his arms and carried her. He leaned down to place her on the sheet where he had turned back the spread.

Her breath caught.

Tension radiated through Carter as he studied her a moment before his arms relaxed and he moved to stand.

This might be her only chance and she planned to take it. Tomorrow she would deal with the fallout. She didn't want friendship; she wanted Carter. Her arms tightened around his neck, bringing him down to her. He supported himself on his hands over her.

"Liz?" He made her name sound like a word of pain and pleasure.

"Yes?" Her lips brushed his.

"Don't play with me," he growled.

She shifted her hips, getting more comfortable. "Who's playing?"

He nuzzled her neck. "I promised you I'd be a gentleman."

"A good host should make his houseguest happy." That was bold. She couldn't believe she'd said that.

Carter pursed his lips in thought and nodded. "That he should."

Liz's heart swelled as he lowered his body to hers. The heaviness felt right. His mouth took hers in a searing kiss.

CHAPTER EIGHT

CARTER HADN'T SEEN this coming. Hoped. Imagined. But the reality—no.

Liz tasted of mint toothpaste and all he could wish for.

As he took the kiss deeper, he ran his hands along Liz's side, following her curves. She wasn't a young woman without dips and rises instead her body had a maturity to it. All full, luscious and desirable. His manhood throbbed to experience all of her.

Hot didn't do her justice when she'd come out of the bath wearing his T-shirt. Where the shirt would've been to the knees on most women, it came high on Liz's thighs. His mouth had gone dry and his length had turned rock hard in seconds.

He shifted more strategically between her legs.

Liz yelped.

Her injured foot. Carter jerked back to sit

on his knees. He could kick himself. "I'm so sorry. I didn't mean to hurt you."

Holding himself in check as Liz maneuvered her foot outside his leg, his breathing caught as she opened her center more to him. "I'm fine. Come back here."

It had been difficult spending the evening with Liz and not touching her. Still, he'd enjoyed their time together. It had been years since he'd had such a worthy opponent at chess. Yet visions of her sleeping in his bed, in his room, in his house kept disrupting rational thought. Only his determination to remain a gentleman had held him in check until now. After all, Liz was only staying the night because she was injured and couldn't drive home.

But she'd reached for him…

He'd not wanted to scare her, or worse, drive her away by pursuing her after he'd promised friendship. Yet now he couldn't stop himself from accepting the invitation. "Are you sure?"

She rested her hands on his forearms and gently nudged him to her. "I like the way you kiss me." Apparently, Liz wasn't timid about her bedroom demands. He appreciated her challenging him; he found it a stimulating surprise.

His gaze locked with hers. "I like kissing you."

She met his gaze. "Then why don't you do it?"

His lips found hers as he slid his arms beneath her, encircling her, bringing her tightly against him. She opened her mouth and her tongue tangled with his in an erotic dance that sent his body into a rage of need.

He hadn't been a monk since his divorce, but he had never been this needy for a woman this fast. He wanted Liz. Only Liz.

She removed her lips from his and nipped at his earlobe.

He shuddered. If he didn't slow them down, he'd be a goner before they ever really started. "Aw, honey, you're killing me."

Her fingers fanned out in his hair as her lips trailed along his jaw.

Carter found the edge of the shirt she wore and pushed it up her thigh. His finger caressed small circles over the smooth skin of her inner thigh. Soon he planned to return to kiss the same spots.

Liz squirmed.

As he touched the edge of her panties, he traced it to the outside of her leg, then slowly returned to her heated center. He brushed his fingertips across the damp material. His jaw clenched as he worked to control his desire.

Liz tugged at his thermal shirt. Together they soon had it removed. He supported himself on his hands on either side of her head while she kissed his chest. His muscles rippled, his hunger escalated. Liz had such power over him. Her hands continued to roam, testing, teasing and tempting. Lowering himself beside her, his hand returned to her thigh.

Traveling up her leg over her hip and then along the smooth plane of her stomach, he reached beneath the shirt. He nudged it higher until a globe of a breast made an appearance. Her nipple strained upward for him. Using his index finger, he circled it. Liz hissed. Slowly he lowered his mouth to surround the erect flesh and tugged gently. Liz rewarded him with a flex of her hips brushing sweetly over his extended length.

Her fingertips gripped his shoulders.

Pushing the shirt to her shoulders, he took in the full view of her ample breasts. Cupping each in his hands, he appreciated their weight, the smoothness. The beauty. He kissed one, then the other before his gaze found Liz's. "You truly are beautiful."

Her hands captured his cheeks and she pulled him to her for a deep wet kiss that drove him mindless. He slid a hand over the curve of her waist, then along her hip, appreciating each dip and rise. When his finger found the elastic of her panties, he pushed beneath to brush her curls. She lurched, then moaned as his finger slipped slowly into her heated center.

His breathing matched her shallow pants.

Liz made sexy sounds of pleasure as he retreated and entered. His manhood pulsed in rhythm to his hand as he mimicked with his tongue his finger's movements. Liz pressed against his hand. Her fingers kneaded his shoulders, begging. She squirmed, shifted, then flexed her body. Her body tensed as her back bowed off the mattress. Her mouth left his. He watched as her head went back, eyes widened in wonder and her mouth formed an O. Her taut hips strained an inch higher. The dam broke on a moan of joy that rolled from her lips. She shook.

"I... I..."

Carter smiled before his mouth found hers again. He'd like to see that reaction to his lovemaking for the rest of his life. He rose from the bed, being careful not to hit her foot.

Liz made a small sound of complaint.

"I'll be right back."

A smile lingered on her lips.

Going to the bath, he found the protection

he searched for and returned to the bedroom. He pulled the bedside drawer open, dropped the extra envelopes inside and slid it closed. With a quick movement, he removed the rest of his clothing.

Liz remained where he had left her with his shirt pushed up over her full and perfect breasts. A daze of wonder lingered in her eyes. Satisfaction filled his chest.

He didn't miss her eyes dropping to study his thick tall manhood as he stood at the edge of the bed. She didn't blush or titter. He could find nothing timid about Liz. Her bold appraisal heated his blood. She bit her lower lip, then the tip of her tongue moved over it. His length twitched, begging to have her. He feared he'd lose it even before he touched her.

Reaching for the shirt, he asked, "May I remove this?"

She nodded and lifted her arms over her head.

Carter tugged it off, then dropped it to the floor. As he did, Liz ran a finger down his swollen length. He watched as her hand encircled him. His breath stuck in his throat.

"So smooth, so strong." She gave him a gentle squeeze. Her gaze flickered to his.

He removed her hand. "And in far too much need of you to have you doing that."

She offered him a seductive grin.

Carter stepped out of her reach, not trusting her or himself. He tore open the package he'd gone after and rolled the protection on. As he placed a knee on the bed, Liz rose to him with open arms, bringing him against her bare heated flesh.

She gave him a wild kiss that had his muscles jumping in his efforts to control his desire. Fearing he might scare or hurt her, his muscles shook to hold himself in check. He moved between her legs. Liz raised her knees, opening wide in invitation. Settling himself in the cradle of her thighs, he shifted until his tip found her heated wet entrance and slid painfully slow into her.

He groaned when he filled her. Looking at Liz, he found her watching him with an earnest expression. Was she afraid of his reaction? "You feel so perfect."

That brought a smile to her lips. She flexed, taking him deeper.

He moved, pulling and pushing. Liz's hips joined him. The tempo increased, heated and became frenzied. As he plunged into her, her fingers cut into the skin of his hips. When he thought he could hold on no longer, Liz's hands dug in and held him to her. He thought he might lose his mind with the pleasure.

She pulled her mouth from his. "Oh, oh, oh," she whispered by his ear.

Liz's grip eased. Satisfaction, bottomless, rich and contagious filled his chest.

No longer able to control himself he thrust hard and deep, completely. Once, twice... He groaned as the force of his release took him to a place he'd never gone before.

His arms and knees weak, Carter lowered himself to her side and closed his eyes.

What had she done to him? He wanted more of this ecstatic rapture that only Liz could provide.

Very few times in Liz's life had she had to deal with the uncomfortable moments after lovemaking. During those occasions she'd not looked the man in the eye. But this time...

She sighed, closed her eyes and absorbed the warmth of Carter. So pleasingly relaxed she couldn't move, nor did she want to. Carter lay along her side, steady and heavy. His breathing had gradually returned to normal. She'd had no idea the languorous feeling she heard about could be real. Romance books touted it, but she'd never experienced it before. Now she understood the big deal other women had made of it. Maybe there was something to the "big hands" theory.

She almost giggled out loud. Melissa would so enjoy learning of this if Liz decided to tell her. Right now, she wanted to savor her time with Carter, share it with no one.

Carter kissed her shoulder, then reached for the covers and pulled them over them. His arm lay across her waist as he nuzzled her neck. "Liz, only an idiot would call you dull. You're amazing."

Something she could only term as love filled her, adding to the warmth Carter shared.

His breathing became even. Carter slept. She followed him.

A large palm skimming over her bare middle woke Liz. It felt so good, perfect. This is the way she always wanted to wake. A fingertip dipped into her belly button before the hand traveled to the curve of her waist and up. A thumb caressing the lower arc of her breast.

Liz absorbed the exhilarating feeling of Carter's hand, of his interest. Already her center pulsed with anticipation.

"I know you're awake." Carter's words tickled the hair at her temple before his lips pressed against it. "I felt your heart rate pick up."

"Just my luck."

"How's that?" His voice rumbled low and sexy as he applied kisses along her jaw.

"To be in bed with such an observant doctor."

His hand traveled lower, brushing her curls. "I like observing you. In fact, I think I'll do more of it."

Liz giggled. Where she'd feared it would be uncomfortable after what they had shared, Liz discovered instead that it was easy, nice. Being with Carter anytime was that way.

Carter rolled to his back, bringing her with him.

"Hey." She opened her eyes and looked at him. The lamp remained on, but out the window it was cavern dark. She had no idea what time it was, and she didn't care. The covers had slipped down her back. "Cold."

"We can't have that." Carter reached around her and pulled the covers over her shoulders. "I rather like what the cold does to you." He lifted her upward. His mouth found one of her extended nipples, circling it, then sucking. He moved to the other breast. "Mmm."

Her womb tightened in the most pleasurable way. No longer cold, she tingled with the need Carter created in her. She ran her fingers through his hair, enjoying his attention. To have a man so fascinated with her body was a new and heady experience. She could get used to it.

Even her ex-boyfriend had spent a minimum amount of time with her in bed. He hadn't lingered, instead dressed and was gone with an excuse he had work to do or needed to get up early the next morning. She'd always wished for moments like this.

Carter's manhood stood tall and firm between them. He wanted her again. To know she created this type of desire in him, again and so soon, empowered her. She rubbed her center along him.

"You keep that up and it'll be all about me and I don't want that," Carter murmured between kisses. Setting her to the side, he twisted until he reached the bedside drawer and pulled out a package. He quickly opened it.

Bolder than she'd ever been before in her life, she took it from him. "Let me do that."

"Be easy with me. I hurt with wanting you."

After she sheathed him, Carter, with his hands on her waist, lifted her. Slowly and, oh, so sweetly she took him into her body. He closed his eyes and appreciated each of her movements. This time their mating remained deliberate. She rode him until she shuddered with delicious release and Carter soon followed. Gradually she came down to rest over him. Carter hugged her close. He had been everything she could want in a lover, willing, giving, caring and exhilarating. She had no idea this bliss existed. A sigh of contentment escaped.

Putting his arm around her, Carter tucked her head on his shoulder. She went to sleep, wishing she could have this forever. Carter, Ryan, they had been whom she'd been searching for.

Dappled light shone through the bedroom window when she woke again. She'd spent the night in Carter's bed, in his arms. She would've never dreamed it possible. Even with his kisses and compliments, she hadn't believed it could happen.

Liz shivered. It was cold. She burrowed further under the blankets, looking for Carter's heat. He was gone. She ran her hand over the area where he had lain. Her heart raced. Panic grew. Had he left because he regretted their night together? Was he waiting on her to come downstairs? Was he thinking of a way to get her to leave?

Liz sat up. Carter's T-shirt lay on the floor and she pulled it over her head. She needed to get dressed, figure out a way to get home. Holding onto the bed, she tried to stand. A painful twinge in her ankle reminded her it had been hurt, but it wasn't more than she could manage. Going downstairs might be a whole other thing though. She carefully started toward the bathroom, applying most of her weight on her other foot.

She'd only been in the bath a few minutes when there came a knock on the door.

"Hey in there. Your breakfast is getting cold." Carter sounded good-humored.

Liz opened the door, still wearing Carter's shirt. Her intention had been to dress in her own clothes before he returned. They would've at least given her some sense of security.

"Mornin'." Carter held a tray loaded with food. He smiled, then headed across the bedroom in the direction of the desk. "Come on, I'm hungry."

He acted relaxed as if her presence in his bedroom happened every morning. Though he wore a T-shirt and sweatpants, he looked all sexy male. In contrast she had become a mass of jitters and nerves. Even in the cool room, he remained barefoot. He had nice feet. In fact, everything about Carter was nice.

Feeling she had no other choice, Liz hobbled after him.

"I see you're making it pretty good on that

ankle." He set the tray on the desk after pushing the books to the side.

She continued to move gingerly toward him. "Yeah, but I won't be running any races. I did make it to the bathroom without a mishap."

He returned to her, giving her a quick kiss on the temple, then guided her toward the cushioned chair. "Good to hear."

"I haven't looked out the window to see how much snow we've had." They kept their slow pace.

Carter helped her into the chair. "There's about four inches."

"Wow." She'd have to stay here a while longer. Maybe it would warm up quick. "As soon as it melts enough for me to get on the road, I'll be out of your hair."

Cupping her cheek, Carter said, "There's no hurry."

She hoped he didn't feel as if he were stuck with her, but she wasn't bold enough to ask him. In fact she wasn't sure she dare say much in front of him in the daylight. She had been last night but now... She shivered from the coolness and apprehension.

"Your nose is red. You must be cold. I'll get you something more to wear."

He hurried to the closet and stopped by the chest for socks. Returning to her, she stood and he helped her into a heavy housecoat. "Sit down and I'll put these socks on you. I forget how drafty this old house can be. It has so little insulation. Ryan and I've learned to wear layers."

Liz pulled the belt tight on the housecoat. Wrapped in warmth and the smell of Carter she felt better already.

"You know, that robe is far sexier on you than me."

Was he just trying to make her feel good? She gave him a weak smile and returned to her chair. "Thanks for this."

"You're welcome." Carter sat in the other chair and lifted her feet to rest on his thigh. He put the socks on her. "Let's have something to eat. I'm starving."

She was, as well. The activity of the night before had worked up her appetite.

"What would you like? I've got cheese, fruit, toast with jelly, of course."

Her stomach growled. "All the above."

Carter looked pleased with her choice. He picked up a small plate off the tray, loaded it with food and handed it to her. "I brought you hot tea but if you'd rather have something else I'll be glad to go down and fix it."

"Don't do that. Tea's fine."

He placed a mug on the desk within her reach. They ate in silence for a few minutes.

"Liz, are you going to ever look at me?"

Hesitantly she met Carter's powerful gaze.

He smiled. "That's much better. Thank you for last night. It was very nice. Better than nice actually."

Some of her insecurity ebbed away. She returned his smile. "I think I'm the one who should be saying that to you."

"Now that we've settled that, how about we finish our breakfast, then let me have a look at your ankle."

Liz nodded and picked up her mug. Between the heat from Carter's look and the tea, her body warmed. Feeling more at ease, she allowed herself to relax some.

When they finished their meal, Carter took care in unwrapping the bandage. The discoloration remained but it hadn't grown.

"I'm no orthopedic guy, but I think I can pronounce this pretty much on the mend." His hand ran up her calf, sending a tingle up her leg to pool at her center. "How about I watch you take a stroll across the floor?"

Liz limped toward the hall door. On her return, she winced. Carter quickly scooped her into his arms.

"You're gonna have to stop doing this.

You'll hurt your back." Liz wiggled in an effort to get down.

Carter's hold tightened. "It's not my back that hurts when you're close. It's another part of my body."

She buried her face in his neck.

"I thought you might like to try out my tub. Have a good soak." He started toward the bath.

"Uh?"

"You know, sit in hot water, bubble bath. That kind of thing."

She raised her head to look at him. "I know what soaking in a bath is. I just hadn't planned to do it in yours."

"I thought since you admired it last night, you might like to try it." Carter put her down beside the bath.

He made it sound like it was no big deal for her to use his tub. He put in the stopper and turned on the water. Soon steam filled the air. He started pulling items out of the chest. "Here's bubble bath. A cloth. Soap is over there." He pointed to a narrow metal tray that spanned the width of the tub. "Can you handle getting in it by yourself?"

"I think I can do that." Liz would rather enjoy having Carter help her, but she wasn't going to admit it. She'd no idea where this relationship might be headed, and she wouldn't take a chance on assuming more than she should.

With a hunger about to surface that he couldn't control, Carter left Liz. Thoughts of her luscious body in his tub was almost his undoing. Just carrying her had him throbbing with need.

Liz had the glow of being well loved when she'd come out of the bath earlier. Her hair mussed, cheeks rosy and still wearing his T-shirt. The only thing that stopped him from taking her to bed again right that moment had been the wariness clouding her eyes. That lack of self-confidence he'd seen when they had first met had returned. So instead of following his body's lead like he'd wanted, he listened to his heart and focused on their meal. When Liz had said she'd planned to put on her clothes, he'd known he'd made the right decision. She'd been planning to run.

At first he'd had no intention of offering her anything more than friendship. In the wake of his disastrous marriage, anything more hadn't appealed to him. He couldn't take chances with his and Ryan's life. Ryan and his welfare would be Carter's sole focus for years to come. Yet a problem persisted and grew the more he spent time with Liz. She'd become increasingly irresistible, important to his life.

He didn't like her being insecure after so much passion between them. Their lovemaking had been indescribably wonderful. He wasn't proud of it, but it had been a long time since a woman's fulfillment had superseded his own. He'd never experienced such desire, pleasure or satisfaction. Emotionally, as well as physically.

Could he be falling for her? He wasn't quite sure what that meant. He had Ryan to consider. He refused to let his son feel like second best. Ryan needed to know he was the most important thing in his father's life. Bringing another person into their world required careful thought. He'd never let his son feel abandoned. Not even for the best sex he'd ever had.

However, there were other things about Liz he found appealing. Her intelligence, the way she ran to help people without any thought of danger to herself, or the fact she'd gone into the medical field to honor her sister's dream, and the way she'd saved the day for Ryan with her creative tree decorations. More than those, he liked the way she had been so touched by something as simple as having a paper handprint hung on a tree.

Without a backward glance, he pulled the

door closed. Instead of focusing on Liz, he tried to keep his thoughts on cleaning up their breakfast dishes. Liz continued to win. After stacking the tray, he carried it downstairs and put everything away.

Returning to the bedroom, he knocked on the bathroom door. "You okay in there?"

"Yes." She paused. "Carter... I need your help."

He opened the door. "What's wrong?"

Liz took his breath away. She stood in the center of the tub, holding a towel over her front as if she'd quickly grabbed it when he entered. A haze of steam hung around her heat-blushed skin. Her hair curled around her face.

"I can't get out of the tub. It's too slippery." She sounded perplexed and embarrassed.

Even with what they'd shared last night, she remained shy about her body. He wanted the bodacious woman who'd invited him into her body to return. The one that made his blood roar.

He walked toward her, his gaze locking with hers. He saw the moment hers widened in anticipation. His fingers trailed through the water. Carter stripped off his shirt. "I could help you out but I could use a soak too. Would you like to stay in just a little longer?"

"I..."

He stepped in front of her with only the side of the tub remaining between them. Starting low on her hips his hands ran up her slick skin to her waist as his lips found hers. Liz trembled. He pulled her closer. Even during his marriage, he'd not been this aggressive with his desire. Just standing near Liz had him hard. "You do know I want you."

"You do?"

Carter stepped back and met her look. "Why would you think I didn't?"

She swallowed. "Because I've always felt I was a disappointment to my partner. You're the first man who hasn't run out on me as fast as he could. I thought the only reason you hadn't was because this is your home and there's snow on the ground."

Carter looked at her for a moment in shock. He wanted to punch something on her behalf. "I'm sorry I failed you."

"How did you do that?" Liz tilted her head in question.

He cupped her face in his hands. "By not making it clear how wonderful I think you are in and out of bed. But I especially enjoyed the bed." He kissed her tenderly.

Sometime later, after cleaning up the water sloshed on the floor, and them both well sated, he and Liz made it back to the bed. The sun had moved high in the sky by the time he opened his eyes. Liz remained nestled beside him.

Something had woken him.

The sound of the phone buzzing drew his attention. He leaned across her to the bedside table and picked it up. Liz moved beside him.

"Hello." He cleared his throat. "Hello."

"Carter?"

He knew the voice immediately. *His mother's.* "Hey, Mom."

"Hi. How're you and Ryan doing?"

"We're fine."

"Are ya'll ready for Christmas?" His mother sounded so cheerful.

"Yeah, we are."

"Good. The reason I'm calling is that your daddy and I would like to come see you and Ryan. Remember, we're flying over to see your brother for the holidays. We wanted to visit with y'all before we left. Celebrate Christmas, you know."

His jaw tightened. He couldn't get out of this. His parents didn't deserve the way he treated them. He just wished he felt more enthusiasm at the idea of seeing them. "Sure, Mom. When should I expect you?"

Liz shifted beside him. With her sensitivity, she had no doubt caught on to the fact he wasn't excited about seeing his parents.

"We'll be there day after tomorrow. In the evening. We'll get a hotel room. We don't want to put you out. We look forward to seeing you and Ryan. We've missed you." The last few words trailed off on a wispy note.

"See you soon, Mom."

He pushed the disconnect button. Staring at a nonexistent spot on the wall across the room, he worked to get his emotions under control. His attitude about his parents was irrational but still he felt it. He would just have to fortify himself for their visit.

Liz's hand touching his arm brought his attention to her. "That didn't sound like a phone call you wanted to take."

"No, it was my mother. My parents are coming for a visit. They want to see Ryan. Christmas and all."

"That sounds nice. I know Ryan will be happy they are coming."

"He will be. I just wish I felt the same. I just hate the way I feel about seeing them."

"Have you ever told them that? I imagine they have noticed something's wrong."

"What am I supposed to say? That they make me feel like a failure whenever I'm around them. They have such a great marriage and mine was such a disaster. That I let them down. I can't say any of that."

"Why not?"

He said nothing for a few moments. "Hey—" he rolled toward Liz "—I don't want to talk about this. I've got to go get Ryan in a little while and I'd rather spend what time I have with you doing other things." He nuzzled her neck and Liz took him into her arms and into her warmth. Nothing but rightness filled him.

CHAPTER NINE

LIZ SAT AT the kitchen table, sipping hot tea while waiting on Carter to return with Ryan. She looked around the kitchen and sighed. A home like this and waiting on two people she loved to return was what she'd secretly dreamed of. Having her own family, a place where she was loved and accepted.

Love. She did love Carter. He was the best man she knew, smart, quick-witted, caring, a great father, the perfect lover. She could find little to complain about where he was concerned. He was everything she'd ever wanted in a man.

Ryan? He was the cherry on top of the sundae. Could Carter possibly feel the same about her?

Despite her insecurities that morning, it had turned out beautifully. Much like how she wished all of her mornings would begin, especially the bathtub experience. If she lived here all the time, it might become her favorite spot to spend time with Carter.

The midday sun streamed through the kitchen window. Melting quickly, the snow would soon be gone and she'd be headed home.

The sound of stomping boots on the front porch brought a smile to her lips. The bang of the front door told her Carter and Ryan were in the house. Liz stood and hobbled into the hallway. The big man and his small replica pulled their coats off and hung them up. Both had rosy noses, pink cheeks and looked like the sweetest candy to her. She had it bad.

"Hey, Liz, you won't believe the snowman I built." Ryan came running and hugged her around the waist.

She returned it and looked at Carter over Ryan's head. Carter smiled that special one she now realized was for her alone. The one that involved a small flame of heat in his eyes. The look that said, *You're special*. Her attention returned to Ryan. "Tell me all about it."

"We even put a scarf around his neck. There's a carrot for his nose."

"That sounds so cool." She looked into Ryan's glowing face.

"I wish I could see it. Is it in the front yard?" Ryan gave her a big nod. "Yes."

"Then I'll go by on my way home and give it a good look. How does that sound?"

That put a huge grin on Ryan's face.

Carter stepped forward and placed his hand on Ryan's shoulder. "Take your stuff up to your room and put it away. There's some hot chocolate waiting for you when you come down. I need to tell you something."

Ryan headed upstairs while she and Carter walked back to the kitchen. When they were in it, Carter grabbed her, giving her a deep kiss.

"I missed you," he whispered across her ear.

She giggled. "You weren't gone thirty minutes."

"Still, I missed you."

The clomp of Ryan's feet on the stairs notified them he would soon join them. They broke apart, both breathing heavier than normal.

Ryan came in the room.

"Have a seat at the table, buddy." Carter pulled out a chair.

"I'll get the hot chocolate," Liz offered, well aware Carter wasn't thrilled his parents were visiting. She moved across the floor with a minimum of pain. Her ankle felt much better.

She listened as Carter told Ryan about his grandparents' plans.

"We'll need to buy them presents," Ryan announced. "We can go to the mall."

"I don't think they're expecting any. They're just bringing you some."

Ryan's voice turned pleading. "It's Christmas. They need presents too."

Liz turned so she could see them.

Carter looked perplexed. "I have to work tomorrow, buddy."

Ryan's face dropped its happy demeanor.

Liz stepped to the table and put her hand on Carter's shoulder for a second. "I have a light afternoon tomorrow. I could take him."

Carter looked at her a moment, then at Ryan, then back at her. Indecision rode clearly on his face. Was Carter afraid to trust her with Ryan? Or was this about his parents?

"All right." He didn't sound completely on board with the idea, but he had agreed. "Why don't I meet you there for dinner?"

Ryan jumped around. "Goodie."

Carter pointed a finger at him. "You have to promise me that you'll do exactly as Liz says."

"I will. Promise."

"All right then, we've a plan." Carter smiled at her. "Thanks."

The next afternoon Liz picked up Ryan at Carter's house. Betsy, the babysitter who they had taken home the night she and Carter met, had stayed with Ryan during the day since he was out of school for the Christmas holidays. Carter had called Liz the night before, letting her know the arrangements. Liz agreed to drive the girl home.

Her and Carter's phone conversation should have only lasted a few minutes but it ended up being two hours long. She savored the call, never having had one like it before. When other girls had been chatting about their long phone calls with boys during high school, she'd been doing homework and reading. She'd enjoyed listening to Carter's deep soothing voice. She sighed at the memory.

She glanced back at Ryan, belted in place in the back seat. This was a first, as well. She'd never transported a child in her car. The fact that Carter trusted her enough to let Ryan go off with her hadn't escaped her. It was a heady and scary feeling at the same time.

As they walked into the mall, she took Ryan's hand. Everything about it felt right. She couldn't imagine having a child and giving it up. She'd fight for her child. Never would she sign away her rights.

"We'd better get busy. We're supposed to meet your daddy at the food court in an hour.

So, what do you think your grandparents might like?" She looked at Ryan.

"Maybe a remote control boat and a puzzle." Ryan grinned at her as if he'd given the correct answer.

Liz chuckled. "I think that's more like what you want. What do you think about a sweater for your grandfather and a scarf for your grandmother?"

"I guess so," Ryan agreed with less enthusiasm than when he'd offered his suggestions.

"There's a nice store right down here. I need to buy my mother something for Christmas too. Let's try it. I think we might find everything we need there."

"Could we get Dad's too?"

"Sure." She'd waffled back and forth about buying Carter a Christmas gift from her. Would they be exchanging presents? She shrugged. It was Christmas. She could give a gift if she wanted.

They started down the mall toward the store she had in mind. Liz quickly learned that Ryan was as full of opinions as his father. She had to make more than one suggestion on gifts until Ryan found what he liked. The gift Ryan found for Carter took the longest but, in the end, Liz believed Carter would like it. They bought a multi-colored sweater for Carter's father, a scarf for his mother and a leather wallet for Carter. Liz had picked out a housecoat and matching house shoes for her mother. Still, Liz left the store disappointed not to find Carter something from her.

It wasn't until they passed a kiosk in the middle of the walking area of the mall selling paintings by a local artist Liz saw what she wanted to get for Carter. It was an oil painting with an angle of the Mooresville's square showing the historical sign, the Brick Church and his home in the background. Perfect.

"Now, Ryan, this picture is our secret from your father. Okay?"

Ryan nodded. "I won't tell."

"Good. I'm going to count on it."

Pleased with her shopping skills, Liz gathered their bags and gave Ryan the smallest to carry. They then, hand in hand, strolled toward the food court. Her heart filled with happiness at the thought of seeing Carter and thinking about how pleased he'd be with the painting.

"There's Dad!" Ryan called. He pulled away and ran to Carter.

Liz's heart leaped. Her gaze met Carter's, who walked toward them with long sure strides and a smile on his face. What would it be like to have Carter look at her that way every day?

When Ryan reached him, Carter gave Ryan a brief hug by putting a hand on his back and pressing the boy against Carter's thigh. He never broke their gaze. As Ryan danced around him, Carter continued toward her.

"Hey." The word came out of her mouth breathy sounding.

"Hi." He pulled her close and kissed her temple. "I wish I could give you a proper hello."

Sweet heat ran through her.

Carter pulled back. "Who's hungry?"

"I am," Ryan announced.

"Me too," Liz said.

A flame blazed in Carter's eyes. "I am too." He took her hand, squeezed it and they headed down the mall.

Was it wrong to wish for forever?

They were almost to the food court when she noticed a middle-aged woman slumped on a bench with an anxious-looking man speaking earnestly to her. He searched the area, then said something more to the woman. Liz pulled her hand from Carter's.

"That woman needs help," she said and hurried ahead of Carter and Ryan.

She reached the couple. "I'm a doctor. Are you all right?"

"Elaine doesn't feel good," the man said, his

face drawn in worry. "She's dizzy and sweaty. She was recently diagnosed with diabetes."

Liz went to eye level with the woman. "Do you have an emergency insulin pen with you?"

The woman shook her head. "I forgot it. It's at home."

"She needs sugar," Carter said from behind Liz. "I'll find some. Ryan, you stand between the end of the bench and the directory and don't move. Take Liz's bags."

Liz gave them to him.

Ryan glanced at the woman, then nodded.

Carter hurried off.

The man hovered nearby. "Sir, could you wait out of the way? She's going to be fine. I promise." Liz sat down beside the woman on the bench. Liz picked up the woman's arm and started taking her pulse.

"Here." Carter handed Liz a piece of hard candy wrapped in a clear cover.

"Thanks," Liz said over her shoulder, as she unwrapped it. She held it to the woman's lips. "Here, you need to put this in your mouth. Suck on it."

She took it.

Liz returned to checking the woman's heart rate. It was elevated. Ninety-six. Liz suspected her blood pressure was high, as well. At least she didn't seem to have a temperature. Liz touched the woman's arm. "Are you feeling any better?"

She nodded.

"Good. The sugar's working. You're still going to need to go to the hospital and be checked out."

The man stepped forward. "I'll drive her."

Carter said, "I've already called 911. The EMTs should be here in a few minutes. I'm a doctor too. We can't in good consciousness let you do that."

Liz looked to find Ryan still waiting where Carter had left him. She gave him a reassuring smile. "Your daddy and I'll only be here a few more minutes."

Soon the emergency personnel were climbing the nearby stairs. A crowd had started to grow around them. While the EMTs worked to get the woman on a gurney, Liz gave them a report.

As the EMTs took the woman away, Carter came to stand beside her. "I can't take you anywhere without you finding some excitement, can I?" Carter put his arm across her shoulders and pulled her against him. "You're amazing."

She smiled at him. "You weren't half bad yourself."

"We make a good team."

She beamed up at him. "The best."

Carter stepped back and looked around the area. "Where's Ryan?"

Liz's head swung to where Ryan had been standing just a few minutes before. Her chest hurt as if it had taken a hit. Ryan wasn't there! The bags still remained on the floor but there was no Ryan.

Fear rose in her throat. She rushed to the sign and looked behind it. *Ryan!* Her pulsed raced. She scanned the area but saw no little boy. All the loss she'd experienced before came flooding back. They had to find him! Her look locked with Carter's. The terror in his eyes matched what she felt. Panic became pain.

"Ryan," she called, circling the area. "Ryan!"

Carter ran to the food court area. His voice boomed around them. "Ryan?"

The area quieted as everyone's heads swiveled in Carter's direction.

"Dad. Hey, Dad. Here I am." Ryan ran up to him.

"Ryan!" Liz yelped, hurrying to them.

Carter scooped Ryan into his arms, hugging him tight. Tears rolled down her cheeks as Liz put her arms around them. Carter opened an arm and brought her in to the circle. They had become her family so quickly.

"I had to go to the bathroom. I couldn't wait any longer," Ryan cried. "I'm sorry."

"Honey, you should've told one of us," Liz said.

"I couldn't get to you."

A security officer joined them. "I was called. I see you have found him."

"Yes, thank you," Carter said.

"I'm glad you have your family together again. You've got a beautiful one. Take good care of them."

Carter nodded. "I will, sir. I promise."

"Merry Christmas then." The security guard walked off.

Carter looked at the food court full of people still watching them, then at Liz. "Why don't we pick up something and go home to eat? I need to settle my nerves."

"Sounds like a good idea."

Carter and Ryan walked her to her car and left to find theirs.

Carter still shook with residual fear that had stayed with him all the way to the house. When he pulled into his parking place, Liz was already there. She stepped out of her car and joined him and Ryan with a drained look on her face.

"Let me have those." She reached into his

SUV to take the two bags from a local hamburger joint. He carried the drink holder and went to the back door. As subdued as he and Liz were, she was thankful Ryan took no notice of it.

As they entered the house and ate their meal, Ryan happily talked about the gifts he and Liz had bought. After their meal, Carter sent Ryan up for his bath.

Liz helped clean away the dinner leftovers, then she walked over to Carter and put her arms around his waist, pulling him close. She lay her head against his chest. Carter wrapped his arms about her and squeezed. He let Liz's big heart and comfort flow into him and ease his anxiety.

"If I had lost him—"

"Shh. He's safe and upstairs." Her hand rubbed his back, soothing him.

"I didn't even check on him during that time."

"I did. He was there. He's a good boy. A very smart one. He knew where the restroom was, and he knew to hurry back. You're a good father. You've taught him well. He's safe, that's what you need to think about."

Carter squeezed her and kissed her temple. They stood like that for a long time.

Ryan called from upstairs. "Hey, Dad, can

Liz come read me a story and say my prayers tonight?"

Carter looked at Liz. She smiled and nodded. "We're on our way up."

As he and Liz walked hand in hand to the stairs, another fear pushed the one over Ryan away. Were he and his son becoming too dependent on Liz?

Liz saw Ryan to sleep. Afterward Liz said she should go. She'd made an agreement with Ryan that she'd take the presents home, wrap them and get them to Carter so Ryan would have them to give his grandparents the next day.

Carter walked Liz to her car. They kissed but mostly they held each other.

During the night his fear of losing Ryan still lingered. Carter wished Liz had been there to hold him, to share his bed. He remembered that moment when he'd seen her and Ryan walking hand in hand with smiles of welcome on their faces toward him in the mall. Everything important in his life came down to them and that moment. His heart had swelled.

He and Ryan were becoming too dependent on Liz for their happiness. Liz wasn't supposed to become this ingrained in his family. He had to put a stop to it. Now, before any of them got hurt more.

Carter slept no more during the night. It wasn't a pleasant decision. His mind kept reliving all those sublime moments of Liz being in his arms, his bed, his bath. Those would be no more. Despite what he knew about her, he couldn't take chances with his heart or Ryan's. Or in hurting her further.

In the middle of the afternoon the next day, his receptionist called back to let him know a Dr. Poole wished to speak to him. Carter didn't want to see Liz today, but she had promised to bring the presents by. He was already too close to his emotional overrun level. "Hey, Liz."

"Hi. How're you doing today?" Sympathy surrounded her words.

"Better. I can at least breathe now."

"Good."

"I have the presents wrapped. I wanted to see if I could bring them by your office after work. Around five fifteen."

She really had gone the second mile. Carter hadn't invited her to meet his parents, not wanting to involve her in something that might turn uncomfortable. They hadn't even discussed doing so. Was she hurt by that? Carter didn't want to know. He didn't want to imply that there was more between them to his parents or to her.

Soon enough he'd be causing her pain for

sure. He didn't like himself much for that, but it was necessary. "I'll wait on you."

"I'll see you then."

The office had emptied out by the time Liz arrived. He waited for her in the reception area. She smiled as she entered, carrying a number of large paper bags with a Christmas design on them. "Hi."

"Hello." He stepped toward her, taking a couple of bags from her. His hand brushed hers. That electricity that had always been between them flashed. He'd miss her with every bone in his body. "Thanks."

She looked hesitant for a second but soon recovered.

Had she expected him to take her in his arms? He wanted to but with what he had to say, he didn't need to lead her on further. "Come back to my office. It was very nice of you to drop these presents off. I appreciate you doing this."

She followed.

He entered his office and walked around his desk, putting it between them. She placed the bags she held in the chair in front of the desk.

"Liz."

Her eyes rose to meet his look. Concern filled them. "Carter, what's going on? Has something happened?"

He couldn't put this off. It wouldn't be fair to her. Taking a deep breath, he said, "I don't see any other way to say it, but this isn't going to work between us."

"I realize I'm the one who stepped over the line, but I thought it was mutual." Her gaze left his and went somewhere left of his head.

"It is, was, mutual. I care for you—"

"Yeah, I get it. I've heard it before," Liz responded, as if she had been expecting those words. She turned, about to leave. He couldn't let her think this was because she wasn't good enough.

"Liz."

She looked at him.

"It's not like that. I just think we've been moving too fast. As much as I've enjoyed the time between us, I just don't see us going any further."

Liz's bottom lip quivered. She bit down on it and nodded.

If he'd been another man, he'd have punched himself. That wasn't what any woman wanted to hear from a man she'd spent the night with. He made himself finish. "I need to focus on Ryan. I had a bad marriage. I'm just not ready to get involved in another relationship right now. I can't afford any more mistakes."

She flinched as if he'd slapped her. He recognized the instant the Liz who handled emergencies with such determination and authority, the one who knew her own mind, emerged. Fury flashed in her eyes. "So now I'm a mistake. How very romantic of you, Carter. You sure know how to sweet talk a woman. No wonder your wife went elsewhere if that's the best you've got."

That was harsh but he deserved. It was Carter's turn to wince. He wasn't handling this well. Or he'd thought Liz would go off into the sunset without any argument. He held up a hand. "Liz—"

She took a step toward the desk. "Oh, no, you're not going to brush me off that easy. Just so you know, I get it. No mistakes allowed. I didn't measure up. Not the first time I've heard that."

Carter started to say something, but Liz went on, "I get that Ryan's mother abandoned him, that you feel you were inadequate in your marriage and that you've disappointed your parents, but I've not done that to you or Ryan. In fact, I've never hinted at doing it. I never would. I'm made of better stuff."

"What matters is I can't trust my thoughts and feelings where you're concerned. What I do, who I do it with directly affects Ryan."

"You can't be there all the time for him," she

snapped. "You can't hover over him. I know that firsthand. My mother has been trying to tell me what to do my entire life. Trying to make me be someone I'm not. After Louisa died, even trying to turn me into her. You're going to have a lonely life if you don't believe in yourself and other people. Sometimes you just have to take a chance. Take my word for it, being alone isn't all it's cracked up to be."

"I'm not alone!"

She glared at him. "What're you going to do when Ryan grows up? Creates his own life, family?"

"You've no idea what you're talking about."

"I've made mistakes. Your parents have made mistakes. Your ex-wife made a colossal one. The difference between me and her is that I would never, *never* give up my child or hurt yours in any way. Or intentionally hurt you. Stop putting your past off on me!"

Carter gaped at her, but she didn't slow down.

"I bet if you think really hard, you might come up with a mistake or two you've made. The thing about mistakes is they have to be learned from, forgiven and not repeated. I don't know what I'd have done differently between us. I've been more of a real person with you than anyone I've ever known. I've

held nothing back. In bed or outside of it."
Liz threw up her hands. "I don't know why
I'm still trying to explain myself to you. Your
mind is made up. You closed it the day you
caught you wife coming in the back door. You
put me in the same basket as her because we
are both female. I can tell for a fact that's all
we have in common. That's a huge basket and
you have a long life not to pick someone out
of it. Either me or someone else. You need to
deal with your issues!"

Carter had heard enough. Liz had given it
to him with both barrels. It was time she heard
a few home truths, as well. He widened his
stance, placed his hands on the desktop and
leaned toward her, ready to go to battle.

"Wait a minute. You sure have taken the
high road when you've got your own demons.
You want me to trust you with my kid, trust
you with my life but you're the one who needs
to learn to trust. To trust yourself. Instead of
being who you are, you're who your sister
wanted you to be. You live your life as an ob-
ligation to her. For example, your work. You're
a good ENT doctor but you're a greater ER
doctor. You're not really doing what you love.
Louisa is still holding you back.

"Or you're conforming to who your mother
wants you to be. You live in the shadows hop-

ing no one notices you, unless an emergency happens, and then you come alive. You're so busy being what others want you to be, you don't know who you really are. You need to step out of the box and stand up for what you want. Be the woman you should be. You let your sister run your life when she was alive. Now you let her memory and your mother run your life."

His chest constricted at the sight of Liz's watery eyes. Her hands went to her ears, but she lowered them again and continued to glare at him.

"You need to decide who *you* are and what *you* want. Start standing up for yourself. There's no reason for you to stay in the shadows. Let your light shine, not Louisa's. You can choose. It's not too late to change."

Liz backed away, shaking her head. "It's just as well we're going our own ways. I was well aware of my issues before I met you. I didn't need you to point them out. Plenty of others already have. The question is, were you aware of yours?" She sucked in a breath. "Thanks for pointing mine out. I'll continue to work on them. Good luck doing the same with yours."

"Liz, you just don't—"

"Hey, I do. I recognize we both carry baggage. That's part of being human. You've had disappointments. I get that. You're just protecting yourself. I have a hard time with rejection. I get that. We don't owe each other anymore explanations. I think we see each other clearly. It was fun while it lasted. Let's leave it at that. I hope you have a good life, Carter. Please tell Ryan the truth about us. I don't want him to think I rejected or abandoned him."

With that, she left his office without looking back.

CHAPTER TEN

EVERYTHING ABOUT THE last few days had been miserable for Liz. She'd barely kept her practice going. Relieved was the only way she could describe her feelings when she closed the office doors the day before Christmas Eve for the holidays. Being merry wasn't in her.

If it hadn't been for her professionalism being so engrained in her, she would've canceled her appointments and closed sooner. The idea of crawling into bed, pulling the covers over her head and not coming out had appealed. There were a couple of problems with that—the largest being it'd give her more time to think about Carter. That she didn't need.

For years she'd had the same routine. Chess and book club, and dinner at her mother's on Thursdays. Today she had to face her mother even though it was so close to Christmas. There could be no deviations on her mother's part. Liz planned to work Christmas morning in the ER for someone with small children so they could be at home with them. Afterward she'd make an appearance for Christmas dinner at her mother's as was their annual tradition.

As the dutiful daughter, she was here on Thursday night, as well. Liz walked up toward the house her mother had kept the same since her father died. Liz pasted on a smile in an effort to show some semblance of happiness, regardless of how she really felt. She entered the front door, knowing her mother expected her, and continued to the kitchen.

Her mother stood at the stove, no doubt seeing to a chicken casserole, spaghetti casserole or pork chops and rice. It had been one of the three for years. They were her father's and Louisa's favorites.

She turned. "Liz… My goodness, Liz, you look awful. You aren't sick, are you?"

"I'm fine." She wasn't, but she wouldn't go into it with her mother.

She pulled a pan from the oven. *Pork chops and rice tonight.* "You know you really should have a more fashionable haircut."

Liz shook her head. She'd just had her hair done a couple of weeks ago. Carter had even commented he liked it.

"I bet you'd have more dates if you did. By

the way, have you thought about going on a dating site?"

Liz held her tongue. Maybe she could eat fast and get out of here before she said something she might regret. That was the problem—she never told her mother how she really felt. "No, I haven't."

Her mother shook her head sadly. "You're not getting any younger."

Carter hadn't thought she was old. She bit her bottom lip. It didn't matter what he thought now.

"If Louisa were here, she'd say you should go out and do things." Her mother placed a bowl on the table.

Liz felt the need to defend herself surging. "I do things all the time."

"I mean where you really socialize with people. Louisa was so well liked."

Liz had stepped out of her comfort zone with Carter and look where it had gotten her. Hurt. Disappointed. In love and heartbroken. Her mother still compared her to Louisa. And found Liz lacking. "Mom, I love you, I do, but Louisa isn't here anymore and I am."

"I know that." Her tone turned sharp.

"I'm not the one you wish had been left behind, but I was. I can't be Louisa. I don't want to be her. You're going to have to accept that."

"I do accept that." Her mother's voice rose in defense.

"Apparently you don't, because you tell me I should be more like Louisa every time we're together."

Her mother let the pan she held slam to the counter.

Liz didn't slow down. What she needed to say was long overdue. "I've gone through my whole life trying to measure up to a sister who's no longer here. When she was alive, it was bad enough but now it's impossible. Louisa is gone. I miss her. I loved her but I can't be her." Liz pointed at her chest. "I have to be me. You're gonna have to take me as I am. Because I'm good enough as I am."

Her mother's mouth gaped. "Liz, I can't believe you're saying all of this. It's not like you."

Liz couldn't believe it either. What she did now was it felt good. Before she'd met Carter, she couldn't have expressed her feelings. He'd given her the confidence to do so. "Until you can take me as I am, we can't have an honest and open relationship. I need you to love me for me."

Her mother moved toward her. "Honey, I do love you. You're a wonderful doctor. A wonderful person. I just want you to be the best you."

Liz stepped back. "I realize that, Mama, but I've got to figure out what's best for me, not you."

"What's gotten into you?" Her mother looked at her with disbelief.

"Nothing. I just need to stand up for myself, be proud of who I am. Not who people think I should be. I can't, I won't, let you or anyone else make me feel bad about myself any longer."

Her mother's face turned worried. "I never meant to do that."

"I know, Mom." Liz softened her voice. "And I shouldn't have let you do it to me. I should've said something sooner."

Her mother stopped before touching her. "I'm only trying to help you. I just don't understand you."

"I don't think you ever have. I don't need you to understand me. I need you to love me. I may never marry and have a family. I've accepted that and you should too. Not harp on it every time we're together."

Her mother looked perplexed and hurt.

Over the last few days, Liz had had enough emotional upheaval to last her a lifetime. She needed to go home and regroup. "Mom, I think you're right. I don't feel good. I hate to leave you with all this food, but I need to go. Wrap it up and we can eat it on Christmas Day."

Liz couldn't leave the house quick enough. She needed to breathe. What she'd said had been liberating but the pain in her mother's eyes still pulled at her. She climbed in her car and drove with no direction in mind.

That brightness she'd felt when she'd been with Carter had left. She'd been dumped and rejected before. She refused to let it define her this time. Or for her mother's view of her to do so, as well. Carter had been right about one thing, it was time she made some changes in her life, set her path toward what she wanted and not be defined by the loss of her sister. She'd start doing that tonight. It wouldn't be easy, but she would continue forward.

The next morning, Liz went to Louisa's grave. She often visited, usually when she felt down. She could talk things out here in the quiet without repercussions. Stepping carefully across the wet grass, she made it to the bench beside the well-tended graves. Her father rested next to her sister. Liz took a seat on the bench and looked at the tombstone that shared her birthday.

Louisa Joanne Poole. Beloved daughter and sister. Gone too soon.

"Hey, Louisa. I'm sorry I've not been by in

the last few weeks. I met a man. A very special man. It didn't work out between us, but I fell in love. He made me realize I'm good enough. That I'm worth fighting for. That I have to stand up and be proud of who I am. He made me see I shouldn't worry about letting you down."

She pushed a tear off her cheek.

"After I lost you, there's been very little happiness in my life until I met Carter. I felt happiness in abundance with him, and his son, Ryan. I've lost it again and I'll learn to live with that but as who I want to be. Not who you thought I should be or who mother wanted me to be."

She wrapped her arms around her waist and rocked back and forth on the bench.

"I've already told Mom everything except about Carter. I just didn't want to go into it with her. At first I was afraid it'd end before it began, then I wanted to keep it to myself because it might end, which it did, and I'd disappoint her once more. When it did end, I couldn't say anything. I hurt her yesterday, but I know we'll get beyond it because I know she loves me. I love her too."

She started to walk off, stopped and turned back to Louisa's grave.

"By the way I saw you tearing up my Christmas ornament. You shouldn't have done that. It hurt me. You were wrong. One more thing— I'm going to give up my practice. I never wanted to be an ENT. That was your dream. I don't mind blood. I'm going into emergency medicine full time. That's what I love and I'm really good at it.

"Wish me luck. I love you, Louisa."

Carter fortified himself against what the next couple of hours in his life would be like. After the scene with Liz, he couldn't imagine it being much worse, until he'd learned his parents had arrived earlier than he'd anticipated.

Betsy had called to let him know. He'd been coming across the river bridge when he received the call. Carter asked if she would ask her parents to pick her up. He didn't want to have to leave again to take her home. He pulled in to his parking area next to a late-model luxury car.

Carter inhaled a deep breath and released it slow and steady. He had to get it together if he planned to get through his parents' visit.

Betsy sat at the kitchen table. "Mom'll be here in a few minutes."

"Please tell her I appreciate her coming for you. I wasn't expecting my parents this early."

"It's not a problem. They're in the living room with Ryan."

Carter handed her some money. "Thanks for watching Ryan this week. You have a Merry Christmas."

"You too."

Life would have to improve significantly for that to happen. He headed toward the sound of voices and laughter. Carter found Ryan sitting between his mother and father on the couch. They were looking at the latest high-demand toy of the season. Ryan face beamed.

"Hello."

They all turned in his direction.

Ryan jumped up and ran to him with the toy in hand. "Daddy, look what Grandma and Grandpa gave me. Isn't it the best?"

"It's wonderful. Did you say thank-you?"

Ryan turned to his grandparents. "Thanks, Grandma and Grandpa."

They both stood and smiled.

Carter's mother said, "You're welcome." She stepped to Carter and opened her arms. "Hi, honey."

Carter hugged his mother.

His father offered his hand and pulled him into a quick man hug. "Hello, son."

"I'm sorry I wasn't here when you got here. I had to stay a few minutes extra at the office."

"No worries, we've been having a good visit with Ryan," his mother said.

Carter looked at his son. "Ryan, run out to the SUV and get the bags out of the back seat. Your presents are in them. You may need help. If Betsy is still here, get her to help you."

"Yay! Liz gave them to you." Ryan ran out of the room.

"Liz?" his mother asked.

"Just a friend." Not even that now, but Carter wasn't going into any of that with his mother and father. He refused to disappoint them more.

"How've you been, son?" his father asked, as he sat back on the couch.

"I've been doing fine." Not true either. "How've you both been?"

"Good. We just miss seeing you and Ryan," his mother said.

"Would y'all like something to drink?"

"I'm good for right now," his father said.

"I'm fine too," his mother said, joining his father on the sofa.

Carter took a seat in the chair near the fire-place.

"We were hoping that when we return, you and Ryan would come to see us for a long weekend? We could catch a couple of basketball games at Memphis State and check out the barbecue places."

"I don't know, Dad. School will be back in and I have work."

Disappointment showed clearly on his parents' faces.

Ryan hurried into the room, lugging the bags with him. He dropped them in the middle of the floor and started reading the tags. "Grandma, this one's for you." He proudly handed her a box wrapped to perfection, including a fancy bow. Liz had done an excellent job, having seen to all the details. Grabbing another, he gave it to Carter's father. "This is yours."

His parents opened the presents with enthusiasm.

His mother pulled the scarf from the box. "Oh, Ryan, I love it. Thank you." She opened her arms for a hug. Ryan went into them. Guilt larger than what Carter usually carried welled in him at the fact he'd kept Ryan from his parents. It wasn't fair to either one of them. Carter should've been better than that. The three of them obviously adored each other. Liz had been right. He needed to get his act together. It was time to clear the air between him and his parents.

His father held the sweater up to his chest.

"Very nice. I'm going to take this on our trip. Thank you so much."

Ryan beamed. "Liz helped me pick them out."

Before his parents started asking questions, Carter said, "I thought we'd go out to dinner. Ryan, you need to go clean up and put on some of your nice clothes. Let me know if you need some help."

"Do I have to wear my nice clothes?" His eyes pleaded.

"Just change into some clean clothes that don't have your lunch on them."

"Okay." He headed out the door.

Carter took a deep breath and looked at his parents. Here went nothing. "I owe you an apology."

"For what?" his mother asked looking perplexed.

"I've been unfair to you both and Ryan because of how I feel."

"Feel?" Again, his mother spoke.

"I know you're disappointed in me and that my marriage ended. You guys make it look so easy and I couldn't hold mine together. Every time we're together, I feel ashamed. I'm sorry I've disappointed you. And sorrier that I've kept Ryan from you. He needs you. I've just recently had it pointed out to me that I have to trust others where he's concerned and that we all make mistakes. I made one by marrying Diane, but Ryan isn't one of those."

His mother was already moving to him. She put her arm around his shoulders. He stood and she enveloped him in a hug that almost stopped his breathing. "Oh, honey, we're proud of you. We know you were destroyed by what Diane did to you and Ryan. We had no idea why you kept pushing us away. We hoped time would make it better. We love you and always will."

His father joined them and hugged Carter, as well. "We've missed you and Ryan."

When his parents stepped back, his father said, "Let me assure you that your mother and our marriage has been far from perfect many times, but with the right person you just keep moving forward. You'll find that right person. I promise."

His mother, with a twinkle in her eyes, said, "If my guess is right, you already have. Maybe that Liz Ryan keeps talking about?"

Anxiety filled Carter. "That's if I can make it right with her again. I may have messed that up too."

His father slapped him on the shoulder. "Humble pie I've found works wonders."

Ryan came back into the room. "I'm ready."

"We are too," his mother said with a bright smile on her face, as she wrapped her arm through Carter's.

A couple of hours later, they were saying their goodbyes in the restaurant parking lot. "I wish you didn't have to leave so soon," Ryan whined.

Carter's mother came to Ryan and gave him a kiss on the cheek, then looked past him to Carter. "I think we'll be seeing more of each other from now on."

Carter smiled and nodded.

"We already have plans for you and your dad to come see us in a few weeks. Will you see that Liz comes with you?" his mother asked.

Ryan eagerly nodded. "I will."

"Now give me a big hug." His mother reached for Ryan. Then took Carter into her arms. "I love you, son."

His father came forward and rubbed Ryan on the head and gave Carter a tight hug.

He and Ryan waved as his parents drove away.

Carter felt lighter, as if he'd dropped a pile of trash he'd been carrying on the side of the road. The evening had turned out better than he would've ever imagined. The only thing that could've made it nicer would've been if

Liz had been there with them. He and Ryan were incomplete without her.

Midmorning of Christmas Day, Liz sat in the office of the Emergency Department doing chart updates on the computer. She moved the small Santa out of the way. Reaching, she picked up a piece of homemade candy sitting on the paper plate she'd filled in the break room earlier.

She glanced out the door to the unit desk with the tinsel lining it and a small Christmas tree sitting on the counter. The staff all wore Santa hats and had even presented her with one. She hadn't felt in the Christmas spirit since she'd wrapped presents for Carter and Ryan. At least helping people today had improved her outlook.

After a short and to the point phone call with her mother, Liz still planned to go to her house for Christmas dinner when her shift ended.

The day had been going smoothly so far. Her cases were much as she'd expected. The usual for holidays. Burns, cuts, sprained ankles and the typical guy who had a heart attack because he thought he was still young enough to play football with his adult kids. Liz had taken care of each one in her stride.

Liz smiled. This was where she belonged. She would miss Melissa and her other office staff when she closed the practice, but she'd see to it they had jobs elsewhere. If she could, she'd convince Melissa to join her in the ER.

She'd come to work with a newfound confidence of knowing she'd be doing what *she* loved. Standing a little taller and feeling a little stronger, she'd begun to like herself.

One of the nurses came to the door and leaned inside. "We've got a case right up your alley."

Liz looked up. "How's that?"

"An acute ear infection."

With a grin, Liz scooted back in her chair. "Those I can handle. I'll be right there."

The nurse smiled. "I thought you would."

Liz took a bite of chocolate fudge and headed to the unit desk. There, she picked up a tablet and checked the pending charts. *Patient: Ryan Jacobs. Seven years old.*

Her heart hammered in her chest. It couldn't be. There must be more than one Ryan Jacobs in the Decatur area. With a foreboding that made her blood run faster, she walked to the exam room. She straightened her shoulders and slid the glass door open.

Ryan lay on the bed. "Liz! It hurts." He

pointed to his ears; his face twisted in a grimace.

Carter stood beside him. "Liz." Her name came out as a surprised whisper.

She ignored Carter and focused on Ryan, moving to the opposite side of the bed from Carter. "Ryan, I'm sorry your ears hurt. I'm going to check you out, then I'll get you all fixed up and stop that pain." She looked directly at Carter. "If your father will let me?"

To her satisfaction, Carter flinched. "Of course, I will."

She watched him a second longer. This wasn't the time or the place to get into it with Carter. They'd said all they needed to anyway. She reached for the otoscope. "I need to look in your ears. This may hurt just a little."

She placed the tip of the instrument in Ryan's ear. He flinched. "I'm sorry. But I need to look in the other one too." She did so. "Yikes you have a double infection. I'm going to give you something for the pain and a prescription for some medicine. You should be good in no time."

Liz turned her attention to Carter. It was so good to see his handsome face, but she couldn't think about how much she'd missed him. "You should consider having tubes put in after the holidays. His ears are badly infected. I'll refer you to a good ENT."

She patted Ryan's leg. "I hope your Christmas gets better."

Carter caught her arm as she stepped toward the door. "Couldn't we make an appointment with you?"

"No."

"I'm sorry about what I said, what I did. I was just scared. I overreacted. I let my past control my here and now. It wasn't fair to you."

"Thank you. I appreciate you saying that," she said politely. As much as she wanted to go to him, he'd hurt her deeply.

"Then you'll see Ryan?"

Liz shook her head. "I can't. I'm not taking any new patients. I'm closing my practice. I'm going into emergency medicine."

"You are?" Carter's voice rose in surprise while at the same time he looked proud of her.

"Yeah, somebody told me recently I needed to make some changes."

"Hey, Dad," Ryan said. "You need to tell Liz he's supposed to go to Grandma and Grandpa's with us."

"You're right, buddy." He turned back to Liz. "My parents would like to meet you." He offered her an unsure smile. "I'd like to introduce you to them too. We're going to see them for a long weekend after the holidays."

Hope filled her. "You talked to them?"

"I did. I cleared the air and they understood. Even better, they still love me. Someone very important to me said I should get my act together. I'm hoping she will forgive me now that I'm starting to." Carter's gaze met and held hers.

Joy she hardly dared to feel filled her.

"Can we talk when you get off? Please?" Carter's eyes begged.

She could make it hard on him, after all he'd hurt her, but he had been right. It was past time for her to take charge of her life. Be who she wanted to be. Apparently Carter had started to make some changes, as well. The biggest deciding factor was, did she love him? She did. Of that she had no doubt.

"I'm supposed to go to my mother's for dinner. But I bet she wouldn't mind you and Ryan joining us. There's always plenty of food."

He glanced at Ryan. "I don't know…"

"I'll tell you what—I'll call her and see if she'd mind packing it up and bringing it to your house."

Carter leaned back in his chair after finishing a full plate of food. "That was wonderful."

Liz's mother glowed.

He had no idea what Liz had told her about them, but her mother was all smiles when she arrived at his house. She'd taken over the kitchen and doted on Ryan during the meal.

He looked at Liz. Her smile reached her eyes. They still needed to talk, but for right now they were sharing their Christmas meal at his kitchen table. Ryan had said he felt good enough to sit at the table and try to eat. What Carter had at this moment was what he'd always wanted in his life, peace and happiness, and Liz brought that into his life.

She gave him a timid look. He loved those, but he equally appreciated those moments when her eyes heated as she took the lead in their lovemaking. Based on his one night with Liz, all of his other experiences with women could be described as bland. She was assertive and sensitive, and very sensual all at the same time. What made it even better was he loved her.

He winked at her. Her cheeks pinked.

He'd loved her when she'd told him how it was. She'd done that clearly at his office and had not backed down when she'd spoken to him at the hospital. He wouldn't be letting her out of his life if he could help it. He needed her, and Ryan needed a fierce mother, as well.

Liz had been there for Ryan more than once. She'd saved the day with decorating the Christmas tree. Again, when he needed someone to show interest in his snowman and as a caretaker when his ears hurt. Ryan should have a wonderful woman in his life, and Carter believed the right one was Liz.

"Ryan, I think it's time for you to get some rest." Carter pushed his chair back.

"If Ryan would let me get him in bed, I'd like to," Liz's mother offered.

Carter looked at him. Ryan nodded. He and Liz's mother were already forming a bond.

She stood and stretched out her hand. "Great. Can you show me your favorite book?"

"Okay."

Carter spoke to Liz's mother. "Ryan can also show you where everything is. A bath can wait until tomorrow."

"Yay." Ryan, with Liz's mom chatting to him, headed into the hall.

Liz rose and began cleaning away the dishes.

Carter stood as well, wrapping his fingers around her wrist. "Leave those. We need to talk."

She nodded. Carter led her into the living room where the only lighting came from the Christmas tree.

"I can't stand it any longer. I've missed you."

He brought her into his arms and his lips found hers. To his relief and pleasure, Liz returned his kiss. A soft moan came from her, feeding his need, but that must wait. Banking his desire, he stepped back. "Come sit with me."

Liz took a seat on the sofa. Carter sat there as well but made sure space remained between them. He wanted them to see each other's faces. Continuing to hold Liz's hand, he faced her, waiting until her gaze locked with his. "I couldn't say everything I needed to say at the hospital. I'm sorry how I treated you. I hurt you and I never meant to. I've let my bad marriage, the enormous mistake of it, overshadow my thoughts and actions. I put that off on you and that was wrong. You're nothing like my ex-wife. You never will be. You didn't deserve how I treated you. I realize that. I was already planning to come to see you. You're the best thing that has ever happened to me. To Ryan." Carter looked deep into her eyes. "I love you. I always will. I'll honor you always. Please just say you'll forgive me."

Liz sucked in a breath. Her eyes widened. Finally she blinked. "Carter, I'm not the person you met a few weeks ago. I thank you for that. You've helped me learn to stand up for myself. To recognize I'm good enough. That

I have my own light to shine in. That I don't need anyone else's approval."

Carter wasn't sure where this was going. He feared she might've realized she didn't need him. She'd said nothing about loving him. He didn't know how he'd survive if she didn't. His hand tightened on hers.

She cupped his cheek. "From now on, when you're scared, promise me you'll talk to me. I'll do the same. It hurts too much to have you reject me."

Carter cringed. His thumb rubbed across the top of her hand. "I can't change the past, but I can make the future different. It'd be easier for me to do that if you were beside me. Will you give me another chance?"

"Silly man." Her fingertips brushed his hair from his forehead as she smiled at him. "If I couldn't, then I wouldn't be here."

"Does that mean you love me?"

Her hands cupped his face. "I've loved you since you came to my rescue in the parking lot of the country club." She kissed him long and deep.

Carter pulled Liz into his lap and poured all his love into his kisses. He broke away long enough to ask, "You'll be mine and Ryan's forever?"

"I can't think of anything I want more."

EPILOGUE

Almost one year later

LIZ SAT ON the sofa in the living room, looking at the Christmas tree lights. She and Carter had spent a lot of time doing that together this year. Ryan had gotten to keep the large ones she'd bought him the year before. In fact, he'd gotten to keep her too.

She glanced at the painting over the mantel. It was the one she'd bought Carter a year earlier. He'd been excited to receive it, even a day late. It meant more to him, and her, now than it had to begin with. They'd been married in the spring in the Brick Church pictured.

Their wedding had been the most amazing one she'd ever attended and the one of her dreams. The sun shone bright, the trees were green with new growth and the dogwoods were filled with white blooms. All of Mooresville attended, along with family and friends.

Ryan had stood tall and important beside his father as best man. Carter's father had honored her by walking her down the aisle. Melissa had served as her maid of honor. She'd worn an I-told-you-so grin the entire ceremony. Her mother had sobbed like a baby. Liz wasn't sure if it had been from happiness, or relief Liz had found someone. Carter's mother hadn't been much better. What really made the day perfect had been Carter standing breathtakingly handsome at the altar, waiting for her. There had been no fear in his eyes, only love.

Ryan ran into the living room, bringing her back to the present. Behind her son was his year-old Labrador retriever, Rex. Liz worked in the ER with someone who had new puppies and Carter had agreed Ryan could have one as a late Christmas present. "Grand said to ask you if I could spend the night with her."

Her mother had come for dinner and had insisted on doing the cleanup. Liz had taken the chance to put her feet up. After a hard and fast day in the ER, Liz gladly accepted the offer. Her mother had embraced being a grandparent as if she'd been made for it, which she had.

Liz smiled. "As long as you promise to help Grand and not make a big mess for her to clean up. Remember, Grandma and Grandpa wil be here tomorrow to spend Christmas with us so you'll need to be home early to see them."

"Okay. Thanks, Mom." Ryan shot toward the door.

Liz liked the sound of that. "Oh, one more thing. I need a hug."

Ryan stopped short, turned and came to wrap his arms around her neck. "I love you."

"No more than I love you." She kissed the top of his head.

As Ryan left, Carter entered. "I was wondering where you got off to. Hiding out from doing the dishes again." He sat down beside her, gathering her into his lap.

Liz snuggled against his chest. She'd found home. "I'm almost getting too big to do this."

"That's not going to happen." Carter's hand caressed her rounded middle. "You'll always be welcome in my lap." The baby kicked. "Apparently Mary Louisa agrees with me." He kissed Liz's temple.

"I think she's going to be as crazy about her daddy as her mom is. I love you, Carter Jacobs."

"And I love you, Liz Jacobs." His kiss proved it.

* * * * *

*If you enjoyed this story, check out
these other great reads from
Susan Carlisle*

Pacific Paradise, Second Chance
The Neonatal Doc's Baby Surprise
Firefighter's Unexpected Fling
Highland Doc's Christmas Rescue

All available now!